GW01036138

TURTLESHELL

To:
Ann and Vic,
Leisa and Andrew

PETER LAWRANCE

TURTLESHELL

AN ALBATROSS BOOK

© Peter Lawrance

Published in Australia and New Zealand by
Albatross Books Pty Ltd
PO Box 320, Sutherland
NSW 2232, Australia
in the United States of America by
Albatross Books
PO Box 131, Claremont
CA 91711, USA
and in the United Kingdom by
Lion Publishing
Peter's Way, Sandy Lane West
Littlemore, Oxford OX4 5HG, England

First edition 1992

National Library of Australia
Cataloguing-in-Publication data

Lawrance, Peter
Turtleshell

ISBN 0 7324 1000 2 (Albatross)
ISBN 0 7459 2435 2 (Lion)

I. Title

A823.3

Cover illustration: Michael Mucci
Printed and bound by The Book Printer, Victoria

Contents

1

Shaun

THE CROW CIRCLED HIGH ABOVE a plain that had been ancient long before the first humans walked across it. On top of a low, bare hill it could see a half-grown boy and, in a dry creek bed nearby, the carcass of a lamb. Several times the lure of sweet pickings tempted the crow to descend, but each time fear of the boy overcame its hunger. So it cried out in frustration and waited, alternately inspecting the lamb and the boy, and scanning the sky for rivals that might rob it of its prize.

Shaun sat very still. Sometimes the soft breeze faded away completely and the dry grass at his feet fell silent. Then he could hear a crow, high in the silver-blue sky, mourning some great loss. He searched and found it, a tiny black speck in the wide, empty vault.

The barren landscape at his feet stretched endlessly

to the south and east, broken in the north by lumpy hills of granite and quartz. To the west he could just make out, through a dusty, grey-green patch of mulga scrub which already wavered in the mid-morning heat, the glint of corrugated iron which marked the workshop and the generator shed. The darker green bulk of a pepper tree beyond the sheds hid the homestead where he lived.

There were times, if he waited patiently for them, when he could hear nothing at all. Absolutely nothing. When the wind was silent and the crow stopped its sad crying, when no ewe called for its lamb and no flight of finches fussed overhead, if no-one was using the generator for washing or welding, there was simply not a sound in the whole world. These moments were thrilling and oddly disturbing at the same time. He couldn't create them; they just happened and he was a kind of audience, listening in to a momentary pause when the whole earth seemed to hold its breath. Sometimes he had the unsettling notion that it was waiting for him, expecting him to do something. But then the moment would pass before he could decide what was required of him and the earth would resume its rustling, murmuring symphony.

From this vantage point, on a rise behind the station buildings, everything he could see to all horizons was Turtleshell. Stupid name for a sheep station, he had always thought, but not as silly as some he knew, like Gluepot or Postmark. The place took its name from a large formation of rock among the hills, which did indeed bear a striking resemblance to the half-buried shell of an enormous turtle when viewed from the south-west at sunset. But he had always cringed a bit when he had to put it on the correspondence school sheets he sent off in the post every two weeks.

Friday would see the last set go with Mum when she drove into town to pick up the supplies. This was Wednesday; he had only today's lesson and one last assessment sheet to complete tomorrow and it would all be over. For *ever*. It was a strange feeling. Although he had always hated being shut in the little classroom for three hours a day, in a funny sort of way he would miss it. Especially the radio sessions, when the crackling voices of classmates, who were spread over thousands of square kilometres, swelled and faded through the static on bad days.

It was nearly December, nearly his birthday. It was weird, he thought. One day he would just wake up and be a year older. He wouldn't be any different really, but somehow this birthday seemed more sig-nificant than others. He thought about this for a while and decided that it was the prospect of going to a real school down in Adelaide next year that made it seem so special.

He shifted slightly to ease the spot where a limestone nodule pressed into his thigh and the crunching of gravel sounded loud to his ears. He had been here for over an hour, he guessed. His mother would be waiting for him, impatient to get school over early in the day, so he should go down before she got too upset and snapped at him in the classroom. He liked it up here, though; here, above the sounds and movement of normal life, where he could see the hills in the distance and vehicle tracks wandering off through endless bluebush like orange chalk lines on a dusty blackboard, where he could look down and see the ant that was his father take an age to walk across the five centimetres of open ground between the workshop and the pepper tree. From here things felt about the right size.

Moving had broken the spell. Shaun stood up and slapped the dust off the seat of his jeans with his hat as he walked to the motorbike. It was blue, with a battered red tank taken from another machine. It was his prized possession and meant a lot to him. It meant he didn't have to beg a lift with Dad or Dave the station hand whenever he wanted to go more than a short distance from the homestead. It meant his father trusted him to look after himself. It meant he was closer to being a man than a boy. He swung his leg over the saddle and then stopped with his heel on the kick-start lever. Somehow, today, it seemed sort of wrong to disturb the perfection of his hilltop with the harsh noise of the motor.

He sat, the machine leaning over to the left because he could only reach the ground with one leg, and looked at the view again. The wind was swinging around through the north on its way to the west, thunderclouds climbing into view from behind the hills. A breeze chilled the sweat between his shoulder-blades and he shivered. He frowned as the thought flitted uninvited across his mind; his life was changing too, swinging to a new direction, and he had no more control over it than over the weather. His father always said that each new season came in with a storm. Well, he was right this time: it looked as though they were in for one last big blow before the month turned and summer arrived.

He pushed off and coasted slowly over the brow of the hill, standing on the footpegs as he wound his way between rocks and bushes on his way down. The only sound was the crunching of limestone under the tyres and the squeaking of the brakes as he controlled his descent.

It was not until he was nearly at the bottom that he kicked the bike into gear and let in the clutch, taking off across the scrubby plain towards the house with a crackling snarl and trailing a plume of dust which blew away to his left before the freshening wind.

2

Joseph

THAT EVENING THEY HAD a visitor. A grinding of gears and a squealing of brakes announced the arrival of Joseph Adams in his ancient Land Rover. Joseph (not Joe, thankyou very much) had been prospecting in the mid-north for longer than Shaun could remember.

From various comments over the years, Shaun gleaned that Joseph used to teach Geology at the University. Eventually he had concluded, he said, that most of his students had heads that would rate about 9 on Mohs' scale of hardness. Now he spent half his time hammering at rocks or digging in creek beds out here. The other half he spent down in Adelaide trying to persuade mining companies that what he had found or what he was about to find was worth paying for.

Shaun liked him; Joseph had a way of making

everything he talked about sound interesting and exciting, and he often brought Shaun unusual things he had found. One of Shaun's favourites was a piece of amber — hard like rock, but orange and transparent like jelly, with an insect perfectly preserved right in the middle. It was a million years old, Joseph had said. The amber had once been sticky gum, oozing from a tree trunk. The insect had become trapped and covered with more gum. Then the tree died and the lump of gum became buried, gradually turning hard and becoming part of the surrounding rocks as they formed.

The prospector always arrived just before tea. Dad often addressed him as 'you old Sundowner', which Shaun had not understood until Joseph explained it to him once.

'During the Depression — oh, before your parents' time — things were really bad. Thousands of blokes were out of work and lots of them took to the Wallaby Track. That meant they walked the country roads with just a swag and a billy, doing odd jobs for farmers and station people in exchange for a bit of food and a bed.

'Now, there were two sorts. Some were really willing to work for what they got, and would camp by the side of the road at night and knock on your door early in the morning, not accepting food or board until they had put in a solid day's yakka. The other sort made sure they arrived at sundown, in time for a feed and a comfortable sleep. That's why they were called Sundowners. Of course, they would shoot through before dawn so they didn't have to do any work.'

'But you're not a Sundowner,' Shaun said. 'You work really hard; I've seen you.'

'No, son,' replied the old man, ruffling Shaun's hair with grimy, callused fingers. 'It's only work if you'd rather be doing something else.'

Tonight, although he talked with Dad all through the meal about sheep and the weather and the price of wool, Joseph kept glancing across at Shaun, eyes twinkling from beneath bushy grey brows. Shaun smiled to himself and wondered what the old Sundowner had brought this time.

Finally, during dessert, he rummaged in his dusty trouser pocket and extracted a chalky rock about the size of a cricket ball which he placed on the table in front of Shaun.

Shaun looked at it, puzzled: it didn't seem very exciting, much the same as any other piece of limestone, and the northern end of the property was just about made of the stuff. The old man chuckled. 'Well,' he said, 'aren't you going to open it?'

Shaun's curiosity increased and he leant forward, examining the rock without touching it. Yes, there it was: a fine crack running horizontally around it, dividing it into two halves. He reached out and gently lifted the upper half off the rock like a lid. Inside, on the surface revealed by the split, was the unmistakable impression of a little fish, every bone of its fins clearly defined in the white rock. Even its eyes and gaping, toothy mouth were distinctly visible. He looked across the table at Joseph, who chuckled again.

'Let's see how much you've learnt from me,' he said. 'Tell me how it got in there.'

Shaun thought for a moment and then took a deep breath. 'It's a fossil. This rock used to be mud at the bottom of the sea. The fish died and sank down into the mud. Then the sea dried up and the mud turned into rock. The fish had rotted away by then, but the shape of it was left inside the rock.'

Joseph grunted with pleasure. 'Near enough,' he agreed, 'except that the sea didn't just dry up. Pressures from inside the earth forced the rocks up from deep, deep in the ocean until they were higher than the sea level. Now the exciting thing about this little fish is that he didn't live in shallow water. No siree, we know this little bloke's relatives, and they live deeper down than you could imagine, further under the sea than the top of Mt Everest is above it. In fact, there are only a few places we know of where rocks formed so far underwater have appeared on the surface.'

Shaun carried the fossil to his bedroom and placed it carefully on the shelf next to the lump of amber. When he returned to the dining room, Dad had just asked Joseph where he was camped this time.

'Up in that gorge in the Turtleshell Range.' When asked what he was working on, he hesitated, frowning. 'I would tell you, except that the mining company I am talking with wouldn't like anyone to know that just yet.'

Dad looked up from his rhubarb and custard, eyebrows raised.

'Then it's a valuable find?' he asked.

Joseph shot him a mischievous glance. 'I know what you're thinking. Well, yes, after all these years of scratching around for peanuts, I think I have finally found something worth finding.'

Shaun went to turn off the generator at the end of the evening. The storm he had felt rising in the morning had broken with a vengeance and he was buffeted by strong blasts of dry air on his way across the yard. Thunder rumbled dully in the distance and crashed overhead. Lightning flickered and pulsed around the horizon like a hundred mad welders. Silhouetted against it, the pepper tree thrashed its limbs in a frenzied dance. The humidity was stifling, but the scent of rain was in the air and Shaun knew the blowing dust at his feet would be damp and fresh in the morning.

Later, as he lay in bed, the old house seemed to talk to him. The roof timbers, laid by his great-grandfather, sighed as the wind leaned on them. A loose sheet of corrugated iron tapped its neighbour on the shoulder. The window pane with its sticker collection chuckled as the storm gusted against it. As the gale increased, bullying the homestead, trying with flashes of lightning to bluff it into lowering its guard, Shaun sank deeper and deeper into sleepy contentment.

There couldn't possibly be anything else in the world he wanted or needed. Except. . . something . . .Well, maybe he would remember in the morning.

3

Sam

THEY DIDN'T ALWAYS GO TO CHURCH on Sundays because it was so far — eighty-five kilometres of mud in winter and dust in summer, and because it was the only day of the week Dad could sleep in if he wanted to.

Mum said it should be a Family Thing and wouldn't go if Dad didn't feel like making the effort. Nobody asked Shaun what he thought, although if they had he probably would have found himself with mixed feelings. He liked getting away from the station and eating a pie or pizza for lunch at the Mobil roadhouse after the service, but he didn't really enjoy church itself.

If he stayed with Mum and Dad in the service he got bored and hot or bored and cold, depending on the season. If he went into the Sunday school lesson, although he liked the teacher, he was older than most of the other children and felt shy and awkward with them. They were all town kids and, while he knew all of them by sight and most of them by name, he didn't feel sort of joined to them the way he did with his radio classmates, many of whom he had never actually met.

This Sunday Dad made the effort. Dave was going to be leaving after Christmas and they were taking on a new station hand. Their minister knew the man's family or something; anyway, Dad was going to meet him after church to finalise the arrangements. If everything was satisfactory, Dave would move temporarily into a room at the end of the shearers' quarters, making way for the new people in the cottage that had been his home for the last three years. Apparently the new hand was married and had a boy about Shaun's age, which everyone seemed to think was an advantage.

The news that Dave was leaving had come as a bit of a shock to Shaun. Although Shaun could remember when he had arrived a few years before, by now Dave had become part of his life, almost like an uncle. His cottage was just across the yard from the homestead and he ate evening meals with Shaun's family five nights a week.

'Where are you going?' Shaun had walked across to the cottage with Dave after work the day he heard the news and had quizzed him through the open door while he showered.

'Bundabilla. North of Olary. Not far really.'

'What do you want to go there for?'

'Cattle. They raise beef as well as wool. I always wanted to work with cattle and this looked like a good way to get into it.'

'But why do you have to go away to do it? Dad's been talking about getting into beef a bit with wool prices like they are. You know that.'

Dave had been silent for so long that Shaun thought perhaps he hadn't heard. Then the water was turned off and Dave stepped out, wrapped a towel around his waist and walked, dripping, across the sitting room to take a picture from the mantel-piece. He showed it to Shaun.

'That's my father. He started his working life at fourteen as a station hand and, when he died at sixty-four, he was still a station hand. I looked at myself in the mirror one day and saw my father looking back.'

He replaced the photo and turned back to Shaun. 'Look, I like this place and I like your dad, but there's no future here for me. There are ten men on Bun-dabilla. Once I get to know cattle better, I reckon I could make foreman, either there or on another place. Maybe I could even manage a station one day. You've got to grow, you know; you've got to change.'

Shaun had grudgingly agreed. If he was going to

be at school next year, he supposed he would not miss Dave so much. 'Do you know the new bloke who's coming?' he asked.

"Fraid not. He's not from around here. Married with a couple of kids, that's all I know. Should be good for you.' Shaun was not sure, and it must have showed. 'Hey, don't take it so hard,' Dave reassured him. 'Between us we've got these sheep pretty well-educated; you shouldn't have too much trouble breaking in a station hand.'

So this Sunday they went to church.

The day started out all right. A pair of wedge-tailed eagles Shaun had seen in the distance several times recently on his rides to the southern boundary had built a nest in a dead tree by the fence not far from the road. He could see it long before they reached the gate, an untidy bundle of sticks with one of the huge, copper-brown birds standing proudly on top of it. Shaun made a long job of opening the gate and actually came to a complete stop after unfastening the chain.

Dad, knowing what had so occupied his attention, let him watch for a whole minute before leaning out of the window and yelling, 'Come on, mate! If you stand there much longer you'll take root. Then they might come and build the next one in your hair!' Shaun grinned at him and swung the gate open to let the car through.

He decided to go into the Sunday school class and that turned out to be the wrong choice. The lesson had already begun when he came in, which made him feel foolish for a start. Then, instead of just letting him slip anonymously into the circle of tee-shirts and jeans on the floor, the teacher felt she had to welcome him like a long-lost son.

'Shaun! How good to see you here again!' (It's only been three weeks for heaven's sake, thought Shaun.) 'Everyone, I think most of you know Shaun from Turtleshell Station.' (Of course they do, thought Shaun; they've all seen me here a dozen times this year except for him over there.) The new boy saw Shaun looking at him and returned a defiant glare.

Shaun decided this was a face he didn't like. It wasn't because it was brown. In fact the Aboriginal features would have looked strong and handsome if it weren't for something that spoiled the effect. Something about the eyes, something wild and hunted. Shaun had once found a feral cat hiding in a dark hole under the woolshed. Stirred with a stick, it had shot out of its refuge in a howling, spitting frenzy of teeth and fur and claws. There was something dangerous about the new boy's eyes. What might leap out if you probed too deeply?

'Right, then.' The teacher's voice jerked Shaun back to reality. 'Who can tell me why we call this time of year Advent?'

They all had to take their shoes off for an activity. At the end of the lesson, Shaun scrambled through the pile of shoes with the rest of the class but couldn't find his.   Finally, while everybody else sat or knelt or hopped about tying laces, Shaun stood in his socks staring at the last remaining pair.   They were blue Dunlops, old and stained, with frayed laces and a hole in one toe. Scanning the room, he saw his own new Reeboks sidling out the door on the feet of the new boy, accusingly white against the brown skin. The teacher was occupied at the other end of the hall, so the only thing to do was to give chase. The shoe thief saw him coming and ducked around the corner of the hall. Shaun grunted with satisfaction: obvious- ly the boy didn't know he was heading into a dead end, trapped between the side of the hall and a wire fence, with his escape blocked at the other end by the back of the toilets.

Several other kids followed Shaun round the corner, curious to know what was going on. Con- fronted by a gathering crowd, the new boy looked around nervously, then sneered. 'What's the matter, can't you take a joke? Here, catch!' He pulled one shoe off his foot and threw it at Shaun, making him duck. Laughing now, he pulled the other shoe off and dangled it by the lace. 'Come and get it if you can!'

The boy let him get right up close, then whirled

the shoe around and let go. Up, up, it sailed in a graceful parabola through the air. Shaun's heart fell as he saw his shoe come down on the roof of the hall, rose as he heard it slither down the steep corrugated iron, then sank again as it lodged with a bang in the gutter, precipitating a shower of rust and flakes of paint.

'Sam Dobson! That will be enough of that, thankyou!' The teacher came belatedly to Shaun's rescue. She made Sam climb up and get the shoe, which was a mistake because all the other kids looked up at him like some kind of hero as he stood at the top of the ladder waving the shoe and yodelling like Tarzan.

After the service, if the weather was fine, the congregation usually stood around outside the church, drinking tea and coffee served by three old ladies behind a wooden trestle table. Shaun found his parents standing by the urn talking to the minister and a woman. The woman was Aboriginal and Shaun guessed she was related to Sam. She carried a pink-wrapped bundle of baby with a tiny coffee-coloured face visible near the top.

'Ah, here's our Shaun,' said Mum, slipping her arm around his shoulder. 'Shaun, this is Mrs Dobson. She is married to the new station hand who's starting next week. You probably met her son Sam over at the Sunday school.' Shaun felt a sort of sinking in the pit of his stomach.

'Your mum and dad been telling me all about Turtleshell,' said Mrs Dobson. 'My husband's, uh, a bit crook. We're staying with a mate of his and, well, they haven't seen each other for a while.' She glanced apologetically at Dad. 'He should be OK tomorrow, though. Then your Dad says we can drive out and get set up in the house.'

Shaun kicked at the gravel, lowering his eyes so she wouldn't notice his annoyance. It wasn't fair, he thought. It was bad enough having to leave next year to go to school; now he had to put up with having his last weeks on the station wrecked. Why did they have to employ someone with a monster of a son like that? They probably expected him to be nice to Sam and play with him and show him around. Well, they had another think coming. It was his land and he was darned if he was going to share it.

4

Dad

MONDAY DAWNED WITH ALL the fresh promise of a glorious day: apostle birds racketed in the pepper tree, Gyp with the one yellow eye ran round in circles barking his delight at the morning, bacon and eggs sizzled on the stove, filling the house with wake-up smells. Shaun was in a bad mood; he was sure life with Sam Dobson was going to be unbearable, and his imagination was hard at work supplying him with reasons to be angry.

By the time Dad had clattered his way through breakfast and pulled on his boots, his son was still poking at the second egg with his knife, watching it slide around the plate until finally it impaled itself on the fork and bled to death.

'All right,' said Dad, 'I give up. What's the matter? Are you sick or is something on your mind?'

Shaun looked up with lowered brows and simply

said, 'I'm OK.'

'Pig's eye you are. You've been getting around like a bear with a sore head since yesterday afternoon. Don't you like being on holidays? We could soon fix up some more school work for you if you like.'

From the other side of the kitchen, Mum threatened her husband with a buttery knife. 'Speak for yourself,' she growled. 'If you think the boy's bored, take him out with you and Dave; it'll only take me a minute to make up another lunch. As for me, I've been looking forward to this day for a long time. I've done my last shift in that classroom and wild horses won't drag me back in there!'

Her smile gave her away though, despite her fierce tone. As they walked across the yard to the sheds, each with his newspaper-wrapped lunch under his arm, Mum called from the door: 'Try not to be too late back: the Dobsons should be here about three,' and Shaun's scowl deepened.

Pulling a bore is a long, back-wrenching, knuckle-skinning process involving a lot of sweating and swearing. To fix the bore pump, you need to raise it from the *bottom* of the bore which can be over a hundred metres down. It is one of the jobs station people love to hate.

First you have to climb up the windmill, immobilise the fan, disconnect the rod and install a block and tackle. Then the pipe with the rod inside is hauled up until the first joint appears and is clamped below the joint to stop it falling back down the bore. The top section of pipe is unscrewed, along with the section of rod inside it, and laid on the ground. Then the tackle is connected to the next section down, the whole process being repeated over and over again until at last the pump appears.

To get it all back, you just do it in reverse, except that by now you are tired and the danger of losing the pump down the hole and perhaps rendering the bore useless is even greater than it was on the way up.

By lunchtime, as the three sat in the shade of the truck, backs propped against the wheels, surveying the neat array of pipes and rods on the ground before them, Shaun's anger had been swallowed up in happy exhaustion.

Dad wiped a smear of mud and rust across his brow with the back of his hand as he chewed his cold lamb and gherkin sandwich. The conversation between him and Dave was suitably laconic, befitting the occasion.

'Mongrel.'

Silence for two minutes.

'Yeah.'

Lunchwrapping rustled as Shaun exchanged his sports page with Dave's comic section.

'Rusted through. Need another length.'

Gyp lifted his head as two wethers came in to drink at the trough, but Dad's raised finger settled him back. A mulga parrot called from overhead.

'Some out at the crutching shed.'

Dave and Shaun both looked at Dad and were rewarded with a good-natured growl. This was a sore point and, though he had long since lost his anger over it, Dad could still be prodded to a reaction. No-one had to say another word: they all knew the story.

Three years earlier, with the mid-north gripped in drought and most dams either dry or treacherous bogs, Dad had decided to sink another bore. There was a small shed used for crutching in the hills near the Turtleshell and, nearby, a spot where water seeped from the ground after rain.

Wally the driller was called in and he agreed that there was an underground stream fed by rain which fell in the hills. He was so convinced that good water was to be found that Dad had bought a new pump, pipe and rods, dismantled the mill at Yinki Dam and carted the whole lot over the hills while the drilling was still in progress. Shaun could remember the creaking, swaying, thumping rig parked by an ever-growing mound of sludge, and the look of triumph on Wally's face when at last they struck water.

The triumph hadn't lasted long. The water was

brackish, too salty even for stock to drink. Somehow, Wally persuaded Dad to let him go ten lucrative metres further and to their relief they struck pure, fresh water. But they still had problems. Although the water was of good quality, it only flowed slowly from the porous rock and could not be pumped at anything like the rate they needed to water the thirsty sheep.

Wally had the solution: blast it. Lower an explosive charge on a string and shatter the strata at the bottom of the bore. 'Works like a charm; done it mobs of times. Water flows in like a beaut.' So gelignite was duly purchased, fused and lowered down the eight-inch opening.

Unfortunately it got stuck about two metres down, then the string broke when they tried to pull it back up. With the hissing of the fuse clearly audible, Wally had run around yelling, frantically looking for a stick to dislodge the explosive. Realising it was too late, he had leapt into the cab of his precious rig and driven it to safety. All Dad, Dave and Shaun could do was scamper back behind the crutching shed and wait with their hands over their ears. . .

'Yeah, there's plenty of pipe at the crutching shed.'

It was a good day's work. They had the rusted length of pipe replaced, new leathers in the pump and the whole ninety metres of it back down the bore by four o'clock. Shaun shinned up the steel latticework of the mill to lower the block-and-tackle to the ground and release the fan from its imprisoning twist of fencing wire. His casual movements belied the fact that less than a year earlier his father had considered him too young to perform this dangerous manoeuvre. Then, bound by the warm fellowship of a job well done, they stood by the truck in silent self-congratulation as the fan spun, the rod creaked and clanked and water splashed once more into the tank.

As though to prove to him that a perfect day could be made even better, Dad nodded his assent as Shaun swung himself up onto the tray behind the cab of the truck, saying, 'I'll ride home with Gyp, OK?' He stood up all the way home, peering forward over the cab, eyes streaming, hair whipping in the wind, the skin of his face massaged by invisible fingers of air.

Behind him, Gyp ran madly from one side of the swaying, lurching tray to the other, barking at everything they passed. 'Gonna *fro* when he should be *to-ing* one day,' Dave was fond of saying, 'and that'll be the end of him: exit one dog.' But Shaun would just grin knowingly and Gyp never put a foot wrong.

5

Decision

THEY CRESTED A RISE that overlooked the homestead on the northern side and, as they bumped down the rutted track towards home, the warm feeling of well-being seemed to evaporate. There was a car parked in front of the house. The Dobsons. Sam. By the time they had run the truck into its shed and replaced the tools in the workshop, a knot of resentment had taken hold of Shaun's stomach. Although he didn't realise it, his face settled back into the same sullen glower with which it had started the day. Dad saw it and stopped in mid-stride, puzzled for a moment. Then he looked across at the Dobson's car and back at Shaun, understanding awakening in his eyes.

'It's Sam Dobson,' he said. 'You don't like him, do you? That's why you were in such a bad temper this morning, am I right?' Shaun said nothing, pushing the toe of his boot savagely into the dirt. Dad frowned, perplexed. He leaned forward, his hands propped on his knees, looking into Shaun's eyes. He often did that when he wanted an honest answer. It was as though it enabled him to see right through and into his soul.

'What's wrong? It's not because he's Aboriginal, is it?' Shaun wanted to tell him what had happened at Sunday school, but it sounded weak and ridiculous now he thought about it, no kind of reason for the animosity he felt towards Sam. He just shook his head.

Dad seemed to lose patience then, and gripped Shaun's shoulders, dark eyes compelling his son's attention. 'Listen, mate, I don't know what you've got against him, but you'd better get rid of it before we walk in that door. Maybe he's got a chip on his shoulder, but has it occurred to you that there might be a reason for that? Sam is going to be living on the property with us and you're just going to have to decide to get on with him.' With that he straightened up and strode away towards the house, ducking under a bough of the pepper tree that most men walked under with room to spare.

Shaun stood at the door of the workshop, willing himself to feel different. He had never disliked anyone as he disliked Sam, and yet it was silly, because he didn't even know him. Other people had stayed at the homestead, even with children of about his own age, and yet he had never felt invaded the way he did right now. All his life the sky and the scrub and the sand, the hills and the stony creek beds, had been so much a part of him that he thought about them no more than he did about breathing. Now that he was close to leaving them to go to school, he was becoming aware of how precious it all was to him. He felt almost as though he wanted to gather up the whole landscape in his arms, to stop Sam's smouldering eyes from seeing it and his hands from snatching it away.

Well, he thought, no-one was asking him to enjoy Sam's company, just to get on with him. He could do that much if he tried. Shaun took a deep breath and set his face in the direction of the house, striding towards the kitchen door with a gait that, had he been able to see himself, he would have recognised as his father's. By the time he reached the verandah he had almost convinced himself he could like the boy.

His mother and the Dobsons sat around three sides of the kitchen table drinking coffee. From his customary spot, standing propped against the angle of the benches in the corner, his father raised an enquiring eyebrow at Shaun and Shaun returned a grim little nod to signal that he was ready to act the part, however difficult it might be.

He was a little surprised to discover that Mr Dobson was white. He supposed there was no reason why he shouldn't be; he just wasn't expecting it, that's all. Mrs Dobson was just saying, 'Y'know, this is a real happy time for me because this is my land; my people come from out this way. I haven't been back since I was a kiddy. We been down in Adelaide, oh, since before Sam was born, and before that we was over Ceduna way.' She had said it was a happy time, but her face betrayed her. She carried sadness like a heavy blanket on her shoulders, and her eyes looked too tired to smile.

Then Mum turned to Shaun. 'I told Sam he might find something interesting to do in your bedroom.' Shaun's mouth opened in alarm, but a warning look from Dad snapped it shut again and he advanced down the passage to face whatever he might find.

When Shaun peered around the doorpost, Sam was kneeling by the bed, doing something with the bedspread where it nearly reached the floor. Hearing Shaun step into the room, he leapt to his feet and whirled around with a decidedly guilty look on his face. Shaun's eyes narrowed suspiciously and, as he stepped forward, Sam retreated a pace and flinched as though he expected to be hit. The model aircraft on the carpet narrowly missed being trampled underfoot. Sam stooped to pick it up and held it out to Shaun. 'I was only looking at it,' he protested.

Shaun faced the intruder angrily. He intended to say something like 'Who said you could touch my stuff?', but the fright in Sam's eyes reminded him of his decision to try and be friendly. Instead he said, 'It's an F-18.'

Sam watched Shaun's face nervously. 'Like on Top Gun? I saw that on TV once.' He turned the plane over in his hands and examined it. 'Take you long to make it?'

'Yeah, days.'

Sam handed the aircraft to its owner and began circling the room, edging towards the door. He slipped out into the passage and a minute later Shaun heard the back door close with a bang that would have earned him a stern reprimand. He went to replace the F-18 on the shelf over his chest of drawers and then stopped, staring at the blank space where the MIG 23 should have been.

He scanned the room and finally located it, one wingtip just sticking out from under the bed. He was not really surprised, when he retrieved it, to find that the delicate undercarriage was broken. It was easy enough to repair, but why had Sam tried to hide it? Shaun was quite sure, now he thought about it, that this was the surreptitious movement he had seen when he entered the room. He shook his head and sighed as he returned the damaged model to its place. He wanted to do what his father had asked and get along with Sam, but it certainly wasn't going to be easy!

All the way down the passage to the back door, Shaun told himself that once he got to know Sam he would like him a bit better. That was what he told himself, but a voice in the back of his head muttered, 'If he tries just one more trick like that, I'm going to get really wild!' Outside he stopped, puzzled, blinking in the glare of the late afternoon sun. Where had that darn kid got to? He walked to the corner of the house and was standing under the pepper tree surveying the empty yard when a sock full of dirt hit him directly on the top of his head.

'Bullseye!'

Shaun picked himself up from the ground, coughing and shaking the red sand from his hair, feeling it trickling down the back of his shirt, and used the strongest word he could think of at the time.

'You mongrel, Sam Dobson! I'll get you for that!' and, as tears of anger wet his lashes — 'Got sand in my eyes now, you mongrel!'

Sam tumbled out of the tree, hooting with glee. 'Let's go and look at the sheep,' he said. 'This is a sheep station, you should have some sheep somewhere. We could round them up. Like dogs. I saw that on TV once. Come on, let's round up the sheep.'

'Muster,' Shaun corrected him.

'What?'

'Muster. You muster sheep, you don't round them up. That's only in cowboy movies.'

'Well muster, then. And we could be cowboys and go after the bad guys while we're mustering the sheep.'

'Don't be stupid. This is a sheep station; there aren't any bad guys on sheep stations.'

'Well, you never know, there could be. Come on, cowboy, let's muster those sheep.'

'They're miles away; over at Two Tanks, the nearest lot.'

'I'm hungry then. Does your mum make biscuits? I asked my mum if your mum made biscuits and she said she didn't know, but she probably would because she lives on a sheep station. Does she make biscuits?'

'Uh, sometimes.'

Sam disappeared around the house towards the kitchen, leaving Shaun completely bemused. You just didn't know where you were with this kid. One minute he was timid and sneaky, the next he was so full of noisy energy you couldn't keep up.

Dinner passed almost without incident, Sam on his best behaviour and Shaun hating him for it. He wished Sam would do something really bad so Mum and Dad could see why he didn't like him, but it didn't happen, and Shaun got into trouble for mixing up the chopped nuts and strawberry topping with his ice-cream the way he had always done.

The cottage wasn't properly set up yet, so Mum

suggested Sam sleep on the folding bed in Shaun's room. Before bed, however, she let them watch a video, which seemed to surprise Sam greatly. He didn't think sheep stations had televisions. On learning that they had a satellite dish behind the house instead of a normal aerial, he made Shaun get a torch and take him out to look at it. Outside, he became aware of the noise of the generator, so they had to cross the dark yard to inspect it. The engine house was full of sound and the warm, sweet smell of oil and diesel fuel. Shaun explained how the motor worked, showing Sam the switchboard and the heavy crank handle hanging on the wall. Sam wasn't sure, but he thought he had seen something like this on TV once.

Walking back to the house, Shaun sensed that Sam was no longer following him and turned to find him standing, head thrown back, staring with open mouth at the sky. Despite the hot day, the night was frosty and clear, and millions of stars burned with cold fire out of the moonless black velvet of the night. As they stood silently staring, Shaun felt for the first time that there might be some hope of being friends after all.

6

Conflict

SAM WAS UP AND RACING before anyone else was awake. Wandering bleary-eyed into the kitchen, Shaun was confronted by the fearsome sight of milk, sugar and corn flakes cascading from the table onto the floor. This was happening, he realised, because the bowl was tipped, and the bowl was tipped because Sam's foot was in it, which in turn was because Sam was standing on the table. Just why Sam was standing in a bowl of corn flakes on the kitchen table was a question too complex for Shaun's early morning brain.

'Whoops,' said Sam. 'I forgot that was there.'

'What on earth are you doing?' gasped Shaun, rubbing his eyes to be sure he was really seeing what he thought he was seeing. 'Mum is going to freak!'

'It's that little lizard,' explained Sam, pointing to a blank spot on the ceiling above the table. 'Well at least it was there a moment ago. You must have frightened it away. Maybe it fell into the sugar.' In a moment he was down from the table and had slopped and squelched and crunched his way across the room with the sugar bowl, and was about to upend it into the sink when Shaun, recovering his wits, leapt forward and prevented him.

'No, believe me, it's not there. I saw it run down the wall and out the door,' he lied. Anything to stop this crazy kid getting him into more trouble than he knew he was already in if Mum came in before the mess was cleaned up. Somehow he knew it would not be Sam who got yelled at.

He got the sponge from the cupboard under the sink and began mopping up while Sam poured himself another generous helping of corn flakes. When his mother did get up, the kitchen was looking healthy enough, but Shaun's day was already mortally wounded. He glared at her when she suggested he might like to show his visitor around the place. (My visitor? he thought: who invited him?) She glared back at him and held the door open.

Shaun set to work showing Sam all the most boring things he could think of — the empty tangle of wire that used to be a chook yard, the stacks of pipe, rod and droppers behind the sheds, the dam, the sheepyards by the woolshed (but not inside where the smells brought back memories of shearing). He was savagely satisfied when Sam thought it was all interesting. He sensed that if he took him to the dump and showed him the stuff he had salvaged over the years, neatly arranged in order of size and shape and what they were made of, or if he allowed Sam onto his hilltop, he would not understand them and would somehow manage to spoil them.

'What do you do here?'

'Pen the sheep up ready for shearing.'

'And what's that over there?'

'That's for dipping. Gets rid of ticks and things.'

'Have you got a skateboard?'

'No.'

'Why not?'

'I don't want one. It'd be pretty useless on the dirt. Got a motorbike, though.'

'Radical! Can I ride it?'

'Don't be stupid; you'd fall off and break your neck.'

'You could teach me.'

Shaun passed over that idea with a silent shudder: there was no way in the world this maniac was ever going to sit on his precious bike!

'What do you do on weekends?' asked Sam.

'Nothing much. Ride around a bit, go to the dump.'

'Sounds pretty boring to me. Do you go into town?'

'Sometimes.'

'What about Adelaide? Do you ever go to Adelaide?'

'What for? My grandparents live in Broken Hill.'

By the time they left the yards by the woolshed, Shaun had had enough. If it was like this after half a day, what was it going to be like *living* with the kid?

Walking back to the house, Sam suddenly said, 'Are there any kangaroos around here?'

'Of course there are,' growled Shaun rudely. 'What do you think?'

'Where are they? Can we go and see them?'

'Why don't you track one? You blacks know how, don't you?'

The moment he had said it he knew he had gone too far, but he was totally unprepared for the reaction. Sam flew at him, fists swinging, yelling, 'Don't you call me black!' Shaun stepped back in fright, catching his heel on something and falling with stunning force on his back in the dirt. Before he could recover, Sam was on top of him, knees in Shaun's stomach, fists battering at his face and arms and chest, yelling over and over, 'I'm not black! I'm not black!' The blows hurt badly, and he could soon taste blood in his mouth and smell it in his nostrils, but the sheer unexpectedness of the ferocious attack rendered him unable to defend himself.

Recovering from the surprise, he began to twist and wriggle desperately, drumming on the ground with his heels and trying to force his forearms over his face. Finally he managed to roll sideways, pitching Sam onto the ground. He scrambled away on all fours, his right hand closing around a short, thick stick as he struggled to his feet. Through a haze of tears he saw Sam coming at him again and raised the stick above his head. He vaguely wondered whether he could actually bring himself to hit him with it, but he never found out, for an iron hand gripped his wrist and his father's voice cut through the roaring in his ears.

'Shaun! What the hell is going on?'

'He started it,' panted Sam before Shaun could answer. 'He was calling me names.'

'Is that true?' asked Dad. Shaun desperately wanted to deny it, to put the argument in a light that would make him feel less ashamed, but in the face of his father's challenging stare he could only grind his toe into the sand and clench his teeth, blinking to fight back more tears. By this time Mum and the Dobsons had caught up with Dad.

Jack Dobson was not as tall as Dad, but thick and muscular like a bull. He seized Sam by the back of his shirt and frog-marched him across the yard to the cottage, the boy's feet barely touching the ground, giving him a vigorous shake every half-dozen steps.

The other three parents stood around awkwardly, each apologising for their boy until Emma Dobson turned abruptly and followed her husband. Then Mum put her arm around Shaun's shoulder and walked him back to the house to attend to his wounds.

Lunch took place in silence. Afterwards, Dad rose from the table muttering something about checking the fence at Four Corners and stalked away towards the sheds. Shaun followed him out the door and stopped. His feet would not take him further because they knew he had nothing to say to his father that would make him proud of him again. He stood miserably in the middle of the road wishing, praying that something would happen to get Sam off the property and out of his life. Mum came over, gently stroked his hair and took him inside to have another look at his eye.

7

Jack and Emma

YOU COULDN'T HEAR MUCH when Jack and Emma fought. It was during the evening when the thumping of the diesel generator covered up the noises. They had been on the place less than two weeks, yet Shaun thought he had heard them three or four times. They would declare a kind of ceasefire when the light bulbs faded through yellow and orange and died as the engine slowed and lisped into silence. Then sometimes you could hear Jack out by the pens roaring at his two dogs to shut up their racket. That was when you knew he was really drunk: when he didn't realise that shouting at them only made them bark louder. Emma's dark skin hid the bruises well enough, but not the swollen eye or the cuts.

It was hard to tell how Sam fared during these bouts; he never spoke about them and Shaun was afraid to ask. The two boys were getting used to one another, but Sam was moody and unpredictable and Shaun concluded that he had inherited his father's temper. Once, however, Sam did not appear for three whole days, and when he did he was limping. Asked what had happened, he just forced a grin and mimed a kick. It seemed Jack had never hit the baby, though.

Tonight was different. The generator stopped but the fighting did not. Shaun could hear it faintly across the station yard, rising and falling, first Jack's bull bellow, then Emma's frightened shrieking. When it did stop Shaun thought it was all over, until he heard ragged, running steps. He knelt on his bed and, with his forehead pressed against the glass, saw Emma stumbling towards the house clutching a bundle to her chest. Although the moon was up, he heard her rasping breath before she was close enough for him to recognise the baby. Its head bounced against her shoulder as she ran, and its arms flopped loosely in the same frantic rhythm.

Mum, still dressed, met her halfway across the vegetable garden, calling to Dad to restart the motor. Dad, just emerging from the generator shed, hesitated only a moment before the urgency in her voice spun him back through the door. He cranked the heavy engine, it thudded back to life, and his long legs had him back to the house almost before the lights had reached their full brightness.

The next few moments were like something out of a movie — except that in a movie you can't taste the fear like stainless steel on your tongue or feel the cold rock of panic pressing up under your ribs. Shaun stood at the kitchen door, clutching the frame, staring with eyes he didn't dare blink. Dad strode to the table, the baby under one arm, and simply swept everything to the floor with the other. Emma was yelling at Dad, trying to get the baby from him and Mum was yelling at Emma, pinning her arms to her sides in a bear hug. Sam had materialised at the back door on the other side of the kitchen and, as their eyes met, Shaun for the first time saw the hard mask dissolve and a frightened child reach out desperately for help.

The baby lay limp on the tablecloth, its knees sort of fallen outwards and its arms spread straight out sideways, palms startlingly white. Dressed only in a disposable nappy, it looked for all the world like a skinned rabbit. The air was warm and the few wisps of damp hair that stuck to the baby's forehead did not hide the large, dark swelling over one eye. For five long seconds that seemed like minutes, Dad did nothing but stand in front of the table and look. Shaun had seen him do that when the truck got bogged, or when he was about to start a complicated welding job. He always said you could save yourself a lot of grief if you took time to think first.

'Phone the hospital,' he said. 'Tell them we're bringing her in.'

Then he began to work carefully and deliberately on the baby. He lifted one little hand and slapped it several times sharply on the back of the wrist. He let it go, and Shaun heard the soft thump as it fell back to the table. He put his ear to the open mouth, then with a worried frown pressed it to the motionless chest. Shaun realised with a start that the baby's lips were distinctly purple. Lifting gently under the shoulders so that the head tilted back, Dad applied his mouth to the little brown face, almost covering it. As he breathed out, the skinny ribs expanded and then collapsed as he removed his mouth, glancing anxiously at the inert body in his arms. Three more times he repeated the cycle, then called to Mum who had reached the phone, 'Tell them we've got a heartbeat, but she won't breathe without help.'

Emma had folded into a crouching position on the floor against the fridge, arms around her knees, shoulders heaving with soundless sobs. Sam tiptoed around the edges of the room to her and knelt beside her with his arm around her shoulders, making soft comforting noises.

Shaun was mesmerised by the battle for life unfolding on the kitchen table, and jumped when Mum shook him by the arm. 'A blanket, Shaun. Get a blanket for the baby. And put some shoes on; we can't leave you here. You and Sam will have to come with us.' Wrenching his gaze away from the table, he ran to his room and pulled the blanket from his bed. Sitting on the floor and pulling on his elastic-sided boots, his mind was a whirlpool of thoughts and impressions. At the back of it all, though, was a sense of gratefulness that he had a mother and a father who could do anything in the world.

The drive to town was strangely unreal, like a dream. Mum sat bolt upright at the wheel with a look on her face that was either fierce concentration or enormous anger. Shaun sat motionless beside her as the dirt road, white in the glare of the headlights, flowed endlessly towards them. The only sound was the muted roaring of the road under the tyres, punctuated by an occasional thump as a pothole appeared from nowhere to hammer the old suspension. Once, a roo whipped past his window, close enough to touch, but it had only flashed for an instant in the bright beam and was gone before Shaun's heart could jump.

Emma had recovered enough to sit with her son in the back seat, holding the baby while Dad continued to breathe rhythmically into its nose and mouth. He must have kept it up the whole way, because when they pulled up under the brightly-lit verandah of the hospital and Shaun twisted around in his seat, he was still at it. People in white coats opened the back door of the car and took the limp form from Dad, while Mum gently helped Emma and Sam from the other side. They all hurried in through glass doors and father and son were left alone. Shaun climbed over the back of the front seat without a word and, when Mum came out an hour later to tell them that the baby was going to be fine, he was asleep with his head on Dad's lap, something he had not done for a long time.

8

Mum

SHAUN SAT ON AN OLD KEROSINE DRUM, staring through the wire at Jack Dobson's dogs. Jack had been dismissed and was apparently 'helping the police with an enquiry'. Sam and his mother were staying with Emma's sister while the baby was kept under observation at the hospital.

Shaun was given the task of caring for Jack's two dogs, but they were a mystery to him. They were totally devoted to Jack, though he kicked them and swore incessantly at them. Now he was gone, their whole reason for living seemed to have left them.

They sniffed and licked at the goat legs Shaun had thrown over the fence, but he knew they would not eat until they were starving. They patrolled the perimeter of their respective compounds, loping tirelessly around inside the wire hour upon hour, pausing only occasionally to cock an ear at noises like slamming doors or car engines.

At night, Shaun knew, they slept restlessly, starting to their feet for no apparent reason to stand quivering, ears pricked, sniffing the breeze for long minutes before settling nervously back onto their filthy potato-sack bedding. If Jack didn't come back for them soon, they would have to be shot.

One slowed its endless pacing and stopped in front of Shaun, facing him from beyond the fence. The moist eyes seemed so lost and lonely that he was tempted to put his fingers through the barrier and scratch the dog's nose. He had done that the previous day and had been rewarded with a snarling lunge, saliva flying from the snapping teeth.

Then a strange thing happened. As he stood, staring at the dog's tormented eyes, Shaun imagined himself standing in the Sunday school hall, peering uncertainly around to meet Sam's sullen face. He smelt again the dust and blood and fear as Sam leapt on him with his dark eyes blazing. An awesome sense of understanding grew in him as he wondered what grief and pain Sam had been through to give him the eyes of Jack Dobson's dogs.

He thought his mother might have laughed at him, but she didn't. She stopped clattering in the sink and waited patiently while he groped for the words to describe the insight he had gained. As he faltered into silence, she leaned forward and kissed him on the forehead.

'Does that make any sense?' he asked, feeling maybe he had gone crazy and imagined it.

'Perfectly,' she replied, smiling with — what was it? — pride? love? 'I know exactly what you mean. Emma has eyes like that, too.'

'Emma said this was her land. That's not true, is it? I mean, I know her people lived here ages ago, but we own it now, don't we?'

His mother pursed her lips and considered her answer. 'Well, not exactly. We own the buidings and the vehicles and so on, but this is a pastoral lease. When we say we own land out here, we really mean we are paying the government for permission to graze sheep on it. Some places are mining leases — companies pay the government for permission to dig up minerals.'

'Yes, but the government bought the land from the Aborigines, didn't they?'

Mum shook her head sadly. 'I'm afraid not,' she said. 'In those days they didn't think the land was being used for anything so they just took it. In any case, I don't think the Aborigines would have sold it if they had been asked.'

'Why not?' asked Shaun. The conversation was beginning to disturb him.

'Well, for one thing, what could we have given them that they wanted? But more than that, I don't think they thought in terms of *owning* the land; it was more a case of the land owning them. They were its caretakers; they looked after it. It's all tied up with their Dreaming, their ancestors, their religion.'

This made Shaun feel a little happier. He could see a way to ease his troubled conscience. 'But our religion is different, isn't it? We don't believe in ancestors or Dreaming stories about the land, do we?'

'Don't we?' queried Shaun's mother. 'How about this one. There was a man who had a vineyard next to the king's palace. One day the king looked out and decided he wanted that piece of land for a vegetable garden. He offered the man a better piece of land, but he refused. The king offered him money for it, but the man said it was not his to sell: it belonged to his ancestors and his descendants. Now, that is part of our religion — it's in the Bible.'

'What happened them?' asked Shaun, although in his heart he was afraid he knew all too well.

'In the end, the king had him killed and took the land anyway. God was pretty angry.'

'Great-grandpa didn't kill anyone to get this land, though, did he?'

Mum ruffled his sandy hair. 'Of course not,' she said.

'Mum,' began Shaun, gaining the confidence to ask her another silly question, 'how do adults know what to do?'

'About what?'

'Well, about things. I mean, you and Dad always know what to do. You make all these decisions and they're right. I mean, like when Emma's baby nearly died, and buying that extra land when the Elders man said you'd be crazy to.' He stopped, not sure how to describe what he meant. 'I had a nightmare once. I was grown up and I suddenly realised I didn't know how to be. I didn't know how to be married or look after kids or anything.'

Mum suddenly threw back her head and laughed. Then she pulled her rubber-gloved hands from the frothy water and hugged him close, wetting one shoulder with her hand and the other with her eyes. Finally, she sat down on one of the wooden kitchen chairs, wiped her nose on her sleeve and looked at him in serious amusement.

'Neither do we,' she said. 'Your dad and I don't know how to be grown up. No-one does. We make it up as we go along. And don't go thinking every decision we make is the right one. We've made some spectacularly bad ones in our time. It's just that we don't talk about them a lot.'

She pulled off the gloves and tossed them onto the sink. Then she placed her hands resolutely on her knees and leaned forward. 'Listen. I was a city girl. Your father was exhibiting sheep at the Royal Show with *his* father when we first met. In time it became clear that, if we were going to get married, either he would have to leave the land and look for work in the city or I would have to give up my dream of becoming a lawyer. It was a really hard choice to make, and I'd be lying if I said I never regretted it.'

Shaun just nodded, unsure of what to say. Mum hesitated before continuing.

'You remember I told you we had two babies who died soon after they were born? That experience hit me very hard. I became very angry. First I blamed your father, then I blamed myself. Finally I blamed the land. It was crazy, I know, but somehow I managed to convince myself that the harshness of the country out here had something to do with the babies dying. I came to hate it — the heat and the dust and the flies — everything about the place made me angry. I nearly left, but I didn't. I knew what that would do to your father.

'I prayed that I wouldn't have any more children, but I became pregnant again. It was the worst nine months of my life. Finally you were born. Alive. I was almost afraid to touch you in case you broke or vanished or something. Every morning, and often during the night, too, I would creep up to your cot with my heart pounding, expecting you to be dead. But you just grew and grew and, well, here you are today.'

Shaun sat opposite his mother in silence, confused emotions chasing each other through his chest. His mother smiled sadly and reached out to push a lock of hair from his eyes. 'The point is,' she said, 'that none of us is ever grown-up enough to know what all the results of our choices are going to be. All we can do is what seems right at the time. As for the rest, well, we just have to trust that God loves us and be thankful for the times he gives us what we need rather than what we ask for.'

The silence was broken by the telephone bell and, as Mum went to answer it, Shaun wandered outside and sat on the step, looking out towards the distant hills without seeing them. Gyp padded across and settled beside him, resting his head on Shaun's knee, pushing his nose into Shaun's stomach until he got a scratch behind the ears. The screen door creaked and Shaun could feel his mother standing under the verandah behind him for a while before she crossed and sat on the step with him. They watched the apostle birds return one by one to the pepper tree for their evening synod and, by some trick of the wind, heard the distant sound of the truck before they saw the dust plume that heralded Dad's return.

'That was Emma Dobson. They want her to take the baby down to Adelaide for some tests, so she asked if it would be possible to leave Sam here with us. That means he would be here for your birthday.' She stopped, looking across at Shaun who said nothing, but nodded slowly as he watched the truck materialise out of the wavering layer of heat on the crest of the hill. It looked as though it was floating above the ground for a while before sinking out of sight into an invisible pool and reappearing further down the hill.

'It's all right,' he said, turning to face his mother. 'I'll cope.'

9

The bike

SHAUN WAS AT THE DUMP when Sam arrived on the mail truck. As he watched the vehicle pull up at the house, he was uncertain how he felt towards the figure that climbed down from the cab. Even from this distance he could hear the door slam and for some reason it made him angry. It was almost a week since Sam had left and he had been enjoying his own company. He had hundreds of square kilometres to move around in, but with Sam's arrival he began to feel crowded.

Shaun didn't go down to the house immediately, but sat for a while in the shade of a rusty water tank, thinking. It was all very well for Dad to order him to get along with Sam, and maybe the kid did have good reasons for acting the way he did, but that didn't make it any easier. He had told his mother he would cope, and he certainly felt sorry for Sam and wanted to help him, but words and feelings were one thing and actions were another. On the other hand, he thought as he swung his leg over the saddle of the motorbike, perhaps it was the other way around: if he acted as though he liked Sam, perhaps the feelings would follow later.

By the time Shaun reached the house, Sam had already been installed in the guest room. He was examining the wardrobe when Shaun came in, and looked up apprehensively.

'It's OK,' Shaun reassured him. 'I won't hit you if you don't hit me.'

Sam looked defiant. 'I didn't want to come. They made me.'

There was an awkward pause as the two stood uncomfortably, watching each other. 'How's the baby?' asked Shaun.

'She'll live,' was the gruff reply. Sam still wore his defiant mask, but he was blinking back the tears.

Shaun took a deep breath and said, 'How would you like to learn to ride the motorbike?' He was horrified to hear himself say it, but he was pleased with the effect it had. Sam first looked surprised, then suspicious, then a shy smile broke through the defensive lines of his face.

It was lunchtime. Informed that they were hungry, Mum told them to make some sandwiches. She hovered within earshot for a while, trying to determine whether she was in for a week of war or peace. Finally she seemed satisfied and asked the boys what they planned to do for the afternoon.

Shaun was a bit sheepish as he announced that there were some places he hadn't got around to showing Sam yet. Mum looked dubious when Sam declared he was going to learn to ride the motorbike, but Shaun nodded agreement and she said nothing. She did say a few things to herself though as the boys slammed out through the screen door, leaving half the contents of the pantry cupboard scattered across the kitchen table.

Outside, Shaun showed Sam where to put his feet on the rear footpegs, warned him to hang on, and headed back up the track to the woolshed just fast enough to impress his guest and just slow enough to keep his mother happy.

Dismounting outside the sprawling stone structure, Shaun propped the bike on its stand and rolled the heavy door aside. The floor in this part was about a metre above the ground outside, to assist in loading the bales of wool onto the truck. They scrambled up and walked inside, their footsteps on the wooden floorboards echoing in the dusty silence.

As far as the work of the station was concerned, this was where it all came together. All the bore-sinking, fence-repairing, dam-checking, trough-cleaning, lamb-tailing and tyre-changing. It all ended with the shearing muster. The yards outside would ring to the barking of dogs, bleating of sheep and the shouting of rouseabouts. The dust would rise up into the sky, turning it pink.

Inside the shed, the particular combination of scents and sounds meant only one thing — shearing. The engine would thump, the shears would whir, the long, wide belt that drove the shaft above the shearing stands would slap and hum with rhythmic urgency. The smell of the wool and the sheep, mixed with the sweat of the shearers and the diesel oil, would produce the sweet aroma that only station people know.

Shaun was not sure he could convey it all to Sam but, as he showed him around and explained the process of shearing, classing and pressing the wool, he began to feel a sense of satisfaction from sharing his world with another person. Finally, after touring the yards and demonstrating the drafting race and the loading ramp, Shaun suggested they go and look at the dump. They clambered back onto the bike and set off across country with Sam hanging on for dear life and yelling 'Radical!' every time they went over a bump.

If Sam was impressed by the woolshed, he was awe-struck by the dump. Shaun had set up a kind of fort made from the large wooden crate the new wool press had arrived in. Hanging from nails on the walls were seventeen hubcaps, all different, that he had picked up along the main road. The best place for finding them, he explained, was a limestone ridge about five kilometres south of the house, where deep potholes lay in wait for unwary travellers.

Sam seemed quite interested in these, as well as in Shaun's collections of bottles, batteries, headlights, telephone-line insulators and sheep and goat horns, but he kept eyeing the motorbike as they moved around the piles of scrap and old car bodies.

'All right,' conceded Shaun reluctantly, 'I'll teach you to ride it. But be careful,' he added. 'Mum will kill me if you hurt yourself, and I'll kill you if you hurt the bike!' He began by showing Sam the gears and explaining how the throttle and clutch worked. After a few tries, Sam managed to get the three controls into good enough harmony to take off fairly smoothly without stalling. After half an hour, Shaun was so pleased with his student that he suggested Sam ride *slowly* back to the house to show Mum.

With Shaun trotting along beside him, Sam puttered proudly into the station yard and up to the front of the homestead. The effect was spoiled slightly when Gyp came bounding up by the front wheel, expecting to find Shaun on the machine, causing Sam to swerve and almost fall off. However, he recovered masterfully and managed a complete circuit of the yard while Shaun called for Mum to come out and watch.

'Tell you what,' said Shaun when he had managed to get Sam off the bike again, 'how would you like to help me move some sheep?'

'What, round them. . . I mean, *muster* them?'

'Sort of. There's a mob of wethers we put into South Mulga Paddock while Limestone Bore was out of action. Now it's fixed, we ought to put them back where the feed is better. Dad's been meaning to do it all week, but he's been too busy with other things.'

'All right, if you reckon we're allowed to.' Sam grabbed the handlebars again. 'Can I ride you there?'

'Better not. We have to take Gyp, so I'd better do it. I'll give you a go when we get there.'

After telling Mum where they were going, Shaun swung his leg over the saddle of the bike and whistled for Gyp. To Sam's delight, the dog came galloping across the yard, took a flying leap and landed with scrabbling claws on the petrol tank in front of Shaun. There he sat, leaning forward with his tongue hanging out the side of his mouth, eyes staring eagerly ahead and his ears back as though they were already blowing in the wind.

Sam took his place behind Shaun and they were away, passing between the generator shed and the workshop before turning onto a track leading east.

10

Mustering

AS THE PASSENGER, it was Sam's job to open and shut the gates. It was quite an education for him, as each gate was a different type and each fastened in a different way. The first was quite straightforward — made of iron piping and fencing wire and fastened by a loop of wire that simply slipped over the top of the gate post.

The second was similar but newer, mainly because a roo shooter had driven through the old one in the dark one night the previous year. This one had a chain with a metal ring on the end attached to the gate post. The chain passed around the frame of the gate and the ring hooked over a big bolt on the other side of the post. It was a bit tight and Sam had to fiddle with it a bit to get it done up again, but eventually it slipped into place.

However, the third gate nearly defeated him. It

was the kind usually called a 'cocky gate'. This is just five twisted strands of fencing wire stretched across the track, with three vertical sticks wired to them to keep them the right distance apart. The whole thing is pulled tight across the opening and held in place by a system that beats everyone the first time. The stick that forms the end of the gate steps into a loop of wire attached to the gate post just above the ground.

At the top, there is a bar about as long as a cricket bat joined to the post by a piece of chain not quite long enough to reach the gate. The bar is passed around the end stick of the gate and pulled back towards the gate post, stretching the wire gate tight, until the end of the bar can be held in place by a small loop of wire hanging on the top strand of the fence. Simple.

Sam made the mistake of unfastening the gate before he understood how it worked. He slid the wire loop off the end of the bar, which sprang away from the fence under the tension of the stretched gate, catching him a painful crack on the side. The gate, released from its fastening, collapsed onto the ground in a tangle of wires and sticks. Well, at least it was open. Sam dragged it to one side to allow the bike past.

'Want a hand shutting it?' called Shaun, as he gunned the bike through the opening.

'I can do it,' was the terse reply.

Sam waited until Shaun was past, with his back to him, before rubbing his bruised ribs. Then he turned to the task of getting the gate back across the track. First he seized the end stick of the gate and began walking towards the gate post. It wouldn't reach. Somehow the wires had become tangled around the sticks so that half the gate seemed to be inside out. Eventually, Sam got them sorted out and tried again.

He got to within a foot of the post, but the gate seemed to be too short. Try as he might, he couldn't pull the end stick close enough to get the foot of it into the loop at the bottom of the gate post, or the bar around the top. His next strategy was to forget about the bottom of the gate and just get the bar through the top. With a grunt of satisfaction, he pulled it tight and slipped the small wire loop over the end of the bar, holding it back against the fence. But that left the bottom of the gate hanging loose and, despite his best efforts, he could not get it into place.

Sitting on the bike watching, Shaun was tormented with frustration. he sensed he should not interfere — just let Sam figure it out for himself — but in the end he could not bear it any longer. He left the motorbike with the engine running and walked back to where Sam was wrestling with the gate. 'Here,' he offered. 'I'll show you.'

Sam swung around with his lips set in a grim line.

'I said I could do it myself!' he grated. 'You think I'm stupid, don't you? Well I'm not! I don't care what you say, I'm not stupid!' Shaun backed off, alarmed, fearing the outburst might signal another attack.

Sam turned back to the stubborn gate and kicked it. He undid the bar and let the gate fall to the ground again. Standing with his hands on his hips, he stared at it, muttering under his breath. Then he began at the bottom. He had discovered the secret: stepping the bottom of the end stick into the wire loop on the gate post, he found he was then able to pull the top of the gate close enough to get the bar around it. Then it was an easy matter to lever the bar back against the fence and fasten it in place.

'Great, you won,' said Shaun, settling himself and the dog back on the bike. 'Now can we get on with the job?' But Sam did not seem to notice.

They found the sheep at South Mulga Dam. As the mill came in sight, Shaun's experienced eyes could pick them out, scattered among the bluebush. He pointed them out to Sam who nodded and smiled, although Shaun had the feeling he couldn't really see them yet. When they were closer, Sam began pointing to them himself and asked how many there were.

'About twelve hundred in this paddock. Most of them are probably around here somewhere, but that tank on the rise over there feeds a trough a few kilometres further on; there are sure to be some there. We'll start at the other end of the paddock and work our way back to here.'

Skirting around the boundary of the paddock, they came to the trough Shaun had mentioned. Sure enough, a dozen sheep were hanging around the water and others were distributed throughout the scrub nearby. The animals began to move away as the motorbike approached but, as they came to the fence, they all turned right and began to dawdle along next to it in single file. Shaun stopped the bike and let Gyp down before dismounting himself.

'Okay,' he said, 'this is what we do. You follow them slowly on the bike. Don't get too close or you'll split them up. Gyp and I will pull in any stragglers and move them over to your lot. When we reach the corner they'll all turn right and follow that fence back to the west. Wait there and I'll show you the next bit.'

Sam was a bit wobbly at first, but he soon remembered the lessons he had learnt at the dump. He was confidently weaving his way in and out between the bushes as Shaun turned and sent Gyp away in a wide circle, designed to gather in any sheep who had not yet joined the mob.

It took about twenty minutes to reach the corner, by which time the number of wethers wandering along in front of Sam had swelled to about two hundred, thanks to Gyp's untiring efforts. For some reason understandable only to sheep, they did not want to turn right at the corner and milled around aimlessly, some obviously contemplating a run for it back past the bike. Sam sensibly did not try to push them and, when Shaun and Gyp arrived, a few practised moves and a shout or two sent them off in their new directions.

The mob was now too big to move along the fence line in single file. Sam's job was to ride back and forth behind them, making sure everyone kept up, while Shaun walked along by the fence. Gyp, as ever, roamed free through the scrub, unerringly picking up any the boys by themselves would have missed.

As they reached the top of a small rise, the mill came into view and then the dam. The sheep around the dam looked up and, seeing their mates approaching, moved towards them. The leaders of the group the boys were driving quickened their pace and the two mobs ran together like long lost friends.

Shaun called Sam over to him and pointed out a gate where they could see the road crossing the fence line on the other side of the dam. He sent Sam around in a wide arc to open the gate, instructing him to include in the circle any sheep he could see in the scrub.

'Just rev the engine a bit,' he said. 'They'll come over and join up with this lot.'

Sam looked pretty pleased with himself when he got back, having added several more sheep to the mob and successfully managed another cocky gate. Shaun had to admit that he was learning fast.

'Now,' he said when they had got the sheep moving down the fence towards the gate, 'this is the tricky part. You have to forget they are individual sheep. Just imagine the mob is a big pool of honey or something, sort of flowing down the fence line. You've got to get it rolling, turning like a wheel. The idea is that when it gets to the gate, instead of going past it, it just rolls on through.'

Shaun was not sure if this explanation made much sense but, once it began to happen, Sam caught on and helped. With a few barks from Gyp, the sheep at the back of the mob next to the fence began to run around the outside, catching up with the others until they reached the front, by which time others from the back had followed them. Soon a pattern was formed which resembled a big, squishy wheel rolling slowly along the fence.

It he had not had Gyp with him, Shaun would have been worried about the possibility that the mob would hesitate at the gate and maybe split up, with sheep running off in all directions, but the dog knew what he was doing. As they reached the gate, the leaders only paused for a moment before rushing on through, pulling the whole woolly tide along behind them.

Sam insisted on shutting the gate and got it first time. He wanted to ride back to the house, but Shaun pointed out that the sun was going down, so they had to move fast if they were going to make it home for dinner. Besides, it was not easy to steer with Gyp on the tank.

As they hummed along the track with bushes whipping along beside them and the sun setting through the trees, Sam said, 'Your dad sure owns a lot of land.'

'He doesn't own it,' answered Shaun.

'Then who does?'

Shaun wasn't sure how to answer. Instead he asked, 'Have you ever been camping?'

'Once we went to a caravan park near the sea.'

'I'll ask Mum and Dad. There's something I want to show you.' they rode the rest of the way home in silence.

At dinner, after Mum had told Dad how well the two boys were getting along and Dad had expressed his approval, Shaun judged the moment was right. He swallowed a mouthful of mashed potato and scratched behind his left ear with his fork.

'Um, I want to show Sam the gorge. I thought we could go up there on the bike and camp overnight.'

Mum looked doubtful. Dad looked thoughtful. To Mum he added: 'We'll be really careful,' and to Dad: 'I think he'd like it there.' Eventually it was agreed that they could go, so long as they *were* really careful. Dad suggested they take one of the radios in case they had engine trouble or found themselves in some other kind of difficulty.

At Sam's request, Shaun slept on the second bed in the guest room, and they lay awake for a long time discussing what they should take on the trip. If it were up to Sam they would need a truck to transport all the food and equipment, but Shaun had done this before and knew that all they needed would fit into backpacks that could be lashed to the motorbike. It would be a bit of a squeeze to get the two of them on, but the ride to the Turtleshell Range was only about half an hour: after that it was all on foot. As they were drifting off to sleep, Shaun had a sudden thought.

'Sam.'

'Mm?'

'Please don't tapdance in your corn flakes tomorrow.'

11

The cave

SHAUN STOOD BACK AND ADMIRED his handiwork. The motorbike was heavily loaded, but Dad had agreed it was safe enough. They had slung the rucksacks, each with a sleeping bag strapped to the top, on either side like saddlebags. The radio had been rolled up in a thick sack for protection and strapped across the handlebars. One of the rucksacks held a plastic container of orange juice but, in addition to that, each boy had a water bottle slung over his shoulder.

Wheeling the machine across the yard to the fuel shed, Shaun held the end of the hose in the tank and gave Sam the job of operating the hand pump on a large drum of petrol. Replacing the cap, he then tied the last item — a flat box containing a first aid kit, some tools and a spare inner tube — to the top of the tank. Back to the house for the mandatory last-minute advice from parents, a moment's hilarious instability while they added their own weight to the equipment on the bike, and they were off.

Waiting just beyond the first gate as Sam fastened it behind them, Shaun surveyed the track ahead, leading towards the range of hills which was their objective. He had lived on the property all his life but, although he knew most of the nearly four hundred square kilometres it covered, he never quite got used to it. Around the homestead you could imagine you belonged, that the buildings and yards were permanent. Somehow, in the rougher country north of the homestead things were different. He could never quite escape the feeling that the land had allowed these man-made inconveniences for reasons of its own, and could just as easily shrug them off and return to its primordial dreaming.

Out there, too, were the animals that avoided the inhabited areas and Sam got his first good look at a kangaroo. They had stopped at a dam. They dismounted and climbed the earth batters around it to check the water level and see that no sheep were bogged in the mud. It was hard to tell who was most startled, Sam or the roo, as they met face to face at the top of the embankment. Recovering its wits, the roo bounded away to the other side of the dam and off into the scrub, joined by a dozen others the boys had not noticed at first. From then on, Sam kept his eyes skinned and quickly became quite good at spotting the slight movement under a tree, or the shape of a head with ears pricked above the level of the scrub.

After passing more gates and checking more dams, they left the lowlands, stitched with creek beds and dominated by bluebush and mulga thickets, and began to climb across broad hillsides of open, dry grassland. As they bowled along next to a fence that stretched straight before them for five kilometres, Shaun pointed out a group of emus away to their right, several adults and about a dozen half-sized young that were running diagonally towards the fence. The gawky birds heard the motorbike but, instead of altering course, they simply ran faster, charging at the fence with heads lowered, powerful legs driving at the hard earth like pistons.

Shaun braked to let them through and Sam nearly fell off the bike laughing as they hit the fence one after another with feathers flying, picked themselves up off the ground on the other side and continued their headlong flight as though following an invisible line ruled across the landscape. Shaun didn't laugh. He had seen too many roo and emu carcasses tangled in the wires, deep furrows beneath telling of their frantic struggles to escape.

Turning through another gate, they began slowly up a rugged, little-used track to the base of the hills.

As they approached the line of rocky peaks, the riding became increasingly difficult, until finally, stopping under a large, shady sheoak, Shaun announced that they had to walk from here. With the motor turned off, they stood for long minutes and let the silence settle over them before unstrapping the packs. Sam looked doubtfully at the rugged rock wall Shaun indicated. He asked what was wrong with the track that climbed to their left towards a gap between two peaks, but Shaun told him it wouldn't take them where they wanted to go.

They shouldered the rucksacks, drank from the water bottles and set off, picking their way over boulders and around thorny bushes, up towards the place where the rock rose almost vertically into the deep blue of the sky. Dry grass swished against their jeans and sticks snapped under their shoes, but otherwise the only sound was their increasingly laboured breathing. The sun rose higher behind them, and sweat was soon running down their faces. Shaun led the way to a place at the foot of the cliff where a narrow crack cut into its face and announced that this was their path to the top.

As they squatted in the shade of a large bush, Shaun pointed across to a shoulder of the hill to their left where a mob of fifty or more goats wound their way upward on some errand or other. Sam was amazed by the range of colours and patterns in their shaggy coats. After seeing so many sheep the day before, Sam asked why they had seen so few on this trip. Shaun explained that you had to know where to look. Although there were about eight thousand on the property, that was only twenty per square kilometre and, if you didn't pass the dam or drive through the area at the time the mob happened to be there, it was possible to cross the entire property and not see even one. They rested for a minute more and then began the climb.

The crack seemed to lead upward for ever. The heat radiating from the granite wall in front of them beat upon their faces and chests almost as fiercely as the sun which assailed their backs. Shaun saw beads of sweat glistening on his bare arms and felt it trickling down his neck to soak his tee-shirt. The straps of the rucksack chafed his shoulders. At this point there was nowhere to go but up, but he knew they were nearly at the spot where the narrow, vertical gash they were following opened out and there was a place you could stop and rest.

He paused and turned around awkwardly, leaning back against the hot granite, wiping his face on his sleeve. Looking down, he could see Sam a few metres below, toiling upward gamely. Sam's curly hair, where it overflowed from under Shaun's spare hat, was plastered to his forehead. His face, as he lifted it to see how far he had to go, was shining with perspiration. Even so, he managed a grin, and it struck Shaun that for all his clowning around, this was the first time he had seen Sam looking genuinely happy. He grinned back before turning once more to resume the climb.

Another five minutes and they had reached the place where the fissure opened out. Over the years, soil had collected here and a few straggly bushes provided a bit of shade. The two boys gratefully shrugged off their packs and wedged themselves into the narrow space with sighs and grunts of relief. They sat for about ten minutes, catching their breath while they raided the packs for biscuits and warm orange juice.

Shaun pointed out the main landmarks: the straight thread of fence that marked the boundary with Morton Vale station, the mill at Matthews Soak just visible above the trees that crowded eagerly around it and, winding away to the south-east, the ochre line of the track they had followed on the motorbike.

The bike itself was not visible from here: the old sheoak where they had left it was close to the foot of the hill, hidden by the curve of the rock. Finally he said, 'C'mon, let's go,' and clambered to his feet, reaching for his rucksack. 'It gets easier from here on.'

'It better,' growled Sam, but he was still smiling.

With grunts and groans about the heat and their aching legs and sore shoulders, they continued on up the hill. It did get easier, as Shaun had promised. The terrain became less vertical and more horizontal as they approached the crest. At last, after detouring around the bottom of a sheer, smooth slab of rock, they scrambled up a narrow winding track and arrived at the top.

This was the highest point on the property and the breeze that fanned it from the west was cool and refreshing. Although he was familiar with the view, it always took Shaun's breath away, perhaps because it was so different from anything else on the station. They stood on the highest of a string of peaks which formed a long, razor-backed ridge, a rampart stretching as far as you could see to the north and south.

Facing them across a valley about four kilometres wide was a matching line of jagged, broken rock walls almost as high. Shaun sometimes thought the whole thing looked as though a huge monster had dragged its claws down a line of hills, stripping them to the bone and leaving a deep scar. Or perhaps it was the ruins of a giants' corridor: the walls were built in many places of great blocks of stone that looked unnaturally square.

As Sam surveyed this spectacle, he gradually became still. His eyes shone as he turned slowly, drinking in the whole panorama from horizon to horizon. At length he said, 'This is a special place.'

'Yeah,' replied Shaun. 'One of my favourite spots.'

'My uncle told me about this,' said Sam. Shaun asked him what he meant, but Sam just looked embarrassed and rummaged in his backpack for a drink. They ate cold lamb sandwiches in silence, sitting on a jutting overhang with their legs dangling in space. Sam only spoke once, to ask about a large dome-shaped mass of rock projecting from the valley floor off to their right.

'Turtleshell,' mumbled Shaun through a mouthful of bread. 'That's what the place is named after. Doesn't look much from here, but it's really big when you get close to it. Finish your lunch; I want to show you something.'

They finished their sandwiches, drank some more of the orange juice and set off again, hiking along the ridge-tops towards the north. Shaun chattered about the first time he had come here with his father, but Sam was unusually quiet, absorbed in thoughts of his own. They slithered down gravelly slopes and laboured up rocky inclines until eventually they stood on top of a sheer cliff directly opposite the Turtleshell.

'Follow me,' ordered Shaun, turning and lowering himself feet first into a narrow crevice that ran back into the rock. Sam peered over the edge then scrambled down, almost beating Shaun to the bottom. They followed the crack down to where it opened into the air high above the valley. Just where it seemed you could not safely go any further, a ledge doubled back under an overhanging brow of rock to reveal a cave deep in the face of the cliff. The crossing was a bit hair-raising with nothing much between them and the valley below, but finally they both stood on the floor of the cave, panting and grinning at each other.

It was only the third time Shaun had been here. He had seen the cave from high on the ridge across the valley late one afternoon when the lowering sun had lit part of the rock face normally thrown into deep shadow by the overhang. It was clearly impossible to approach from below and he had set about trying to find a way down from the top.

His perseverance paid off when he noticed a goat emerging from the crevice and wondered where it had been. He was sure nobody had been to the cave for a long time. Probably nobody else in the world even knew it existed, he thought, and he had decided not to show it to anyone. It was going to be his most private place in the world. All the way from the homestead he had debated with himself about whether to show Sam the cave. He nearly hadn't but, seeing Sam's reaction, he was glad he had.

The cave was almost completely round. Even the floor was curved like a shallow dish, and the roof arched overhead, making the inside higher and wider than the circular opening. It was like an enormous bubble frozen in the granite. The first time he had been inside he had recognised it as an excellent place to camp: it had a magnificent view out over the valley to the mountains beyond. It was sheltered from sun, wind and rain, and it was impossible to roll out in your sleep as the floor rose towards the front.

Lying on his stomach at the mouth of the cave, Sam grinned approvingly when Shaun untied his sleeping bag from its place on the rucksack and unrolled it in the centre of the floor. He grunted his thanks when Shaun handed him a biscuit, then resumed his watch, prone, with his chin resting on his folded arms, gazing out over the valley as the shadows lengthened and the sun sank behind the peaks. Shaun set up the little gas cooker he and Dad used during the fire-ban season from November to March and opened a tin of sausages and vegetables. By the time it was ready, the far ridge was just a jagged silhouette sharp against the red-orange of the sunset.

Long after the last purple glow had faded, they lay awake, wrapped in their sleeping bags. The clear sky, framed in the opening of the cave, was a radiant mist of stars which wavered as it soaked up the heat of the day. The moon as it rose behind them gradually illuminated the ridges opposite, revealing their massive forms far more dramatically than the sun had during the afternoon. Some of the rocky outcrops seemed to sparkle in the cold, white light, while their shadows were so black they might have been bottomless holes in the mountainside.

Sam spoke, answering the question he had avoided earlier. 'Whenever I visit my uncle, he tells me all this Nunga stuff. You know, Aboriginal things. Dreaming stories like the Rainbow Serpent and all that. He used to come from around here.' Sam sat in silence for a long time. 'I reckon Aboriginal people used to come here in the old days, don't you?'

Shaun thought carefully before he replied. 'Well, I think that if I was Aboriginal and I lived around here, I would come here a lot. You're right: this is a special place.' That thought seemed to please Sam, and he smiled and rolled over with a contented sigh. The moon slowly rose high enough to light the floor of the long valley. The sound of the car which bumped along the rough track towards the southern end around midnight floated up to their cave, but it was too faint to disturb their sleep.

12

The shooting

THEY ATE TOAST AND VEGEMITE for breakfast. At least it was supposed to be toast. Shaun held it over the little ring of gas flames with a fork and it ended up as warm bread with a circle burnt onto each side. Neither of them minded, though, and they demolished a dozen slices between them before turning to the biscuits.

It was Sam who first noticed the approaching vehicle. 'Hey, give me the binoculars,' he demanded, leaning dangerously far out over the lip of the cave. Shaun handed them over, urging him not to drop them. Sam fiddled with the focus for a moment and then peered intently southwards. 'I thought it might be your dad, but it's not: it's a different sort of car. Land Rover, I think. Going pretty fast by the looks of it.'

By the time Shaun had persuaded Sam to relinquish the binoculars, a second dust trail had come into view. Shaun studied them each in turn and frowned. It *was* a Land Rover; he was sure it was Joseph Adams' aged vehicle. And yes, it was travelling very fast, much too fast for safety. It lurched and bounded along the twisting, rocky track and Shaun could now hear the motor howling in pain as it fought its way up the rising ground towards the Turtleshell.

Turning his attention to the following vehicle, Shaun saw that it was a battered white Ford ute. It too was moving at a furious pace, faster even than the Land Rover. The distance between the two decreased until he could see them both in the field of view at once. It almost seemed that he was observing a race. . . or was it a *chase*?

With growing alarm, Shaun watched the Land Rover gain the crest of the rise and disappear from view behind the great grey dome of the Turtleshell before re-emerging on the far side. Jolting and sliding, it careered downhill now, the canvas flap at the back waving and snapping with every bounce. The white ute rounded the Turtleshell and, to Shaun's relief, slid to a halt in a cloud of dust on the other side.

He was just beginning to feel a bit silly for imagining Joseph was in danger when the doors of the Ford opened and two figures jumped out. His stomach twisted into a hard knot when he saw that the passenger was carrying what could only be a rifle. The armed man climbed quickly onto the back of the ute and leaned forward, resting the rifle barrel on the roll bar behind the cab.

Sam was jostling Shaun's arm, demanding to know what was going on, but Shaun watched, dumb with horror, as the ghastly drama was played out in the valley below him. The distance between his vantage point and the vehicles, together with the restricted view through the lenses, gave it an atmosphere of unreality. The marksman fired, worked the bolt and fired again and again. Each time, a tiny puff of white smoke appeared at the muzzle of the weapon and Shaun found himself counting them. There were four in all and, as the third appeared, the sound began to reach their ears, echoing over and over from the rocky facets on both sides of the valley until the separate cracks mingled and merged into a single noise like enthusiastic applause before fading away.

The firing must have lasted only a few seconds, but it seemed longer. Shaun suddenly swung the binoculars to the right, desperately trying to locate the Land Rover. He glimpsed it blurring across his vision, swung the lenses anxiously back and settled on the moving target. The vehicle had almost reached the creek bed at the bottom of the slope, but it was swerving alarmingly to the right and left, crashing through bushes as the driver wrestled it back onto the track.

As it reached the creek, Shaun could see it was going too fast. He found himself pressing his foot into the ground as though he could transmit the force by sheer willpower to the brake pedal of the vehicle. The Land Rover almost made the final turn before the creek, but entered the crossing on the wrong line. It threw a shower of sand and small rocks into the air as it nose-dived into the dry bed and rocketed towards the further side. It hit the bank on an angle, climbed vertically amid a fountain of dust and clods of earth, then settled back almost peacefully onto its right side.

Sam was silent. He had heard the shots and seen the horrified expression on Shaun's face. Shaun lowered the glasses, stunned, and turned towards the other boy, shock and anger in his eyes. 'They shot him,' he whispered. 'They shot Joseph.'

Sam took the binoculars from Shaun's unresisting fingers and trained them first on the Land Rover in the creek bed and then on the ute almost directly below them. 'Whoever they are, they're not hanging around to see how he is. They're off back the way they came.'

Shaun hardly dared to ask. 'Joseph,' he breathed, 'can you see him? Is he OK?' Sam stared through the lenses for a long time before he lowered them and shook his head. Shaun leapt to his feet and began frantically searching through the rucksacks, throwing the contents haphazardly around the cave, muttering fiercely under his breath.

Suddenly he turned on Sam and grabbed him savagely by the front of his shirt. 'What have you done with the first aid kit?' he demanded, tears running freely down his cheeks. When Sam reminded him they had strapped it to the handlebars of the bike, he swung away and began kicking the rucksacks, furious at himself for leaving it behind.

Sam seized him by the shoulders and began shaking him, shouting his name. Shaun twisted from his grasp with a snarl and raised his fist to defend himself before he realised the light in Sam's eyes was not anger but concern. He stopped his ranting and sank onto the dusty floor with his chin in his hands.

Sam looked at Shaun sadly for a moment and then said, 'Tell you what else is still with the bike: the radio. That'd be helpful, but I don't think we've got time to go back and get it. We ought to check on Joseph first. If he's still alive, we can still help him. There must be something we can do.' He thought for a moment. 'We'll need water and one of the sleeping bags. We'd better take some of the spare clothes: we might be able to use them for bandages or something.' He began picking out items from the mess on the floor and stuffing them into the larger of the two rucksacks. 'Can you get down into the valley from here?'

Shaun wiped his eyes and sniffed. 'Uh, I don't know. I mean, I've never tried, but it would be pretty hard, I think.'

With Sam leading, carrying the rucksack, they stepped carefully over the lip of the cave and ginger-ly felt their way back along the ledge to the spot where the crevice cut back into the face of the cliff. They debated for a moment about whether to climb up to the top and see if they could find a way down further north, but Sam noticed that the ledge con-tinued on the other side of the crevice, much narrower and dipping steeply downwards as it curved out of sight around a shoulder of the cliff. He shrugged the pack from his back and, before Shaun could protest, dropped to his hands and knees and began inching backwards down the steep path until he disappeared around the curve.

Suddenly there was a shout from behind the bulge of granite and Shaun's heart nearly stopped. Not until Sam's shining brown face emerged again two minutes later did Shaun realise that he had been holding his breath. 'You stupid idiot!' he gasped, the air exploding from his burning lungs. 'You scared the life out of me!'

'Come on! Grab the pack, there's a way down!' With that, Sam vanished again and Shaun had no choice but to shoulder the rucksack and shuffle backwards onto the precarious shelf.

It was one of the most frightening things he had ever done. Only the thought of Joseph lying injured in the wrecked vehicle, and the knowledge that Sam had come this way without falling off, kept him creeping resolutely backwards. He lost sight of the crevice that could lead him to safety as he backed around the curve. He could not see behind him and one glance out into the void on his right made his heart pound like a diesel generator and his vision blur, so he fixed his gaze firmly on the patch of rock in front of his eyes.

As he concentrated on moving his hands and knees one by one backwards down the steep gradient, the thought occurred to him that Sam had done it without hesitation and without the benefit of knowing someone had accomplished it safely before him. Gradually, the downward angle of the ledge increased and he began to feel his knees slipping, but just as the panic began to rise in his chest, he felt Sam's hands grip his ankles and guide his feet onto a firm footing.

Shaun's legs felt wobbly, barely able to support him, and he leaned against the hard granite wall while the waves of nausea and shivering subsided. His tee-shirt was soaked through with perspiration and he marvelled that Sam could still look calm.

Recovering, he looked around and saw that they were about halfway down a steep cut similar to the one that led to the cave, but wider, biting deeper into the cliff and opening much further down the mountain. The bottom of it was filled with loose shale, chips and flakes of rock that had fallen from the sides over the years. It looked like a frozen river of gravel sloping down to the mouth of the crevice. Following the cleft with his eyes, he saw that the shale fanned out as it left the cut and ended on the lower slopes of the valley not far from the Turtleshell.

They had to jump about a metre down to the gravelly floor of the crevice and they did it together. The moment their feet hit the shale, however, it began to move. First it was just the rocks under their shoes, then, as they sank up to their ankles in the unstable mass, the stones around them began to slip downwards, too. Shaun clutched desperately at the sides of the cut, but they were too far away. The boys were being carried downwards at a rapidly increasing speed and the ledge they had leapt from was soon far above them.

It became harder to stay upright and the weight of the pack on Shaun's back threatened to over-balance him. He sat down in the rolling, sliding bed of stones and, to his surprise, found it almost comfortable. He was beginning to enjoy the ride. He looked at Sam beside him and slightly above, and found that he had done the same. Sam tried to say something, but the hissing and clattering of stones drowned his words as the whole floor of the crevice swept downwards, carrying the two boys with it.

Suddenly, the moving walls on each side opened out and then disappeared from view as they shot out into the valley. The rocky cataract subsided and slowed until they came to a stop, laughing weakly and coughing in the dust that hung in the air.

'Wow!' gasped Shaun when he found his voice. He lay back in the shale and twisted around to look at Sam.

Sam grinned back and waved. 'Hey, that was great! Want to go again?'

13

The crash

THE EXCITEMENT GENERATED BY THE WILD RIDE down the mountain soon faded, overtaken by morbid imaginings of what they might find at the site of the crash. The two boys hurried as best they could over the scrub-covered ground towards the creek. Shaun kept looking anxiously south in the direction the white ute had taken, afraid that the two men might decide to return.

He was relieved when they reached the creek about half a kilometre up from the crossing: jumping down into the dry bed, they were able to move without obstruction as well as being out of sight of the track.

The sun was well above the hills now, heating up the enclosed corridor of the gorge. Shaun was tiring. His breath came in ragged gulps and the rucksack bouncing on his back made balance difficult in the sandy creek bed. He began to get a stitch, but kept trotting forward, clutching his side to relieve the pain. The twists and turns of the watercourse were frustrating. He expected each bend to reveal Joseph's vehicle, but the next stretch was always empty, leading him to wonder whether they were even in the right creek.

Suddenly, there it was. The Land Rover lay with its right side against the bank of the creek, nose angled into the sky, left wheels off the ground. There were deep scars in the sides and bottom of the creek where the vehicle had ploughed through the earth and the left front mudguard had been bent right under by the impact, tearing a long gash in the tyre. There was no sign of Joseph.

The boys approached apprehensively, circling the Land Rover, eventually getting close enough to peer into the cab. It was empty. Sam scouted around, presumably for footprints, while Shaun, gathering up his courage, got down on his hands and knees and looked into the narrow space between the side of the car and the bank. At least Joseph wasn't trapped there, but where on earth *was* he?

The hair on the back of Shaun's neck began to prickle and he looked nervously around at the trees and bushes that grew up to the edges of the creek. Despite the increasing heat of the sun, he shivered. The two boys met at the back of the vehicle and looked at each other. Sam shrugged wordlessly.

Shaun took one corner of the canvas flap and pulled it aside to look in. He nearly screamed, and stumbled back against Sam as Joseph lunged forward, wielding a large tyre lever.

They all froze, the boys in shock, Joseph in amazement. Then he sank back against the chaotic jumble of equipment, weak with relief. When he was able to speak, he said, 'Thank God it's you! I thought they had come back for me.' Then, without another word, he closed his eyes and slumped over sideways, the tyre lever slipping from his fingers. Shaun climbed awkwardly into the tilted back of the truck and scrambled forward to where Joseph lay. In the light that filtered through from the cab he could see bruises on the old man's face. Also, two more tyre levers had been strapped to his right leg with bandages that were now soaked with blood.

Sam crawled in beside him and let out a low whistle. 'What do you think?' he said. 'Should we move him?'

'No choice,' decided Shaun. 'We can't leave him here; he needs a doctor. And besides, those men might come back.'

'So how do we get him to the house. . . on our backs?'

Shaun hesitated. 'I don't know. We'll think of something. But first, help me get him out of here.'

Together the boys slid Joseph down to the back of the Land Rover. The tail gate had buckled in the crash, and they had to kick it repeatedly to move it, but in the end it sprang open and they carefully slid the old man out onto the sandy ground. Shaun tenderly supported his injured leg and Sam, reaching under Joseph's shoulders and around his chest, dragged him backwards into the shade of an over-hanging acacia.

Though in his sixties, he was solidly built and heavier than he looked, but they managed it. Shaun retrieved the water bottle from the rucksack and gently bathed Joseph's face. He was rewarded by a groan and the grey eyes flickered open.

'Thank God it's you,' murmured the old Sundowner again after Shaun had coaxed him to drink a little. 'How did you get here, anyway?'

Shaun and Sam, interrupting each other in turn, explained about the camping trip, the cave and how they had witnessed the shooting. 'Who are they?' asked Shaun when they had finished. 'And why did they want to shoot at you?'

Joseph grunted. 'I'd give a lot to know who they are myself. I reckon I know what they're after, though. Last week I went down to Adelaide to register a claim and talk with a mining company. Perhaps I looked a little too pleased with myself when I got back to the hotel where I was staying.

Shouted drinks for the bar. Those two must have followed me back up here thinking I had found something worth stealing.

'I woke up this morning to find them going through my stuff in the back of the Landy. They grabbed me when I challenged them and started to knock me around. They tried to tie me up, but I got away and took off in old Laura here.' He looked affectionately across at the battered vehicle and sighed. 'Nearly made it, too, didn't we, darling.'

Shaun had been studying the Land Rover. At the end of Joseph's story he got to his feet and walked over to it, fingering the ripped tyre and trying to open the bonnet. He could see no bullet holes; all the damage seemed to be from the crash itself. Finally he returned to where the others were watching him from the shade.

'We have to get her back on her wheels,' he said. Joseph and Sam made no reply so he continued. 'Those men might come back; we have to get you out of here. We can't carry you and you certainly don't look as though you could walk very far. There's a radio with the motorbike, but that's on the other side of the hills. No, I reckon the Land Rover is the only way to move you.'

Joseph pursed his lips and shook his head grimly. 'Even if you could right it and change that tyre,' he said, 'there's no guarantee the motor is still in running condition after a smash like that.' He had begun to hold his injured leg between his hands. Now he sucked in his breath and screwed up his face, sweat breaking out on his forehead.

Shaun, spurred on by Joseph's distress, scrambled back through the tailgate and began to rummage around in the piles of gear. He didn't quite know what he was looking for; just something that might be useful, anything that might help them manhandle the heavy vehicle back into an upright position.

A moment later, he saw it and grunted with satisfaction. He pulled the hand winch back out into the open and called for Sam to help him. Together they hooked the end of the cable securely to the door pillar on the upper side of the Land Rover. They had to ask Joseph how to free the ratchet that prevented them from unwinding the rest of the cable, but eventually they had it extended across the creek to a young tree anchored firmly in the bank. Joseph told them where to find a length of chain and they soon had the winch attached to the tree.

Then began the slow, laborious job of winding in the cable. They took it in turns to push back and forth on the lever. At first it was not too hard as the winch took up the slack cable and pulled it taut, but from then on it took both of them, one pushing and one pulling. Shaun was about ready to give up when they noticed the first definite movement. The nose of the Land Rover slipped an inch or two down the bank and the sight of it gave them renewed strength.

Gradually the upward angle of the vehicle changed until it was almost level, though still leaning over against the bank. Shaun looked into Sam's shining dark eyes and saw in them a spark of life that had not been there before. They grinned at each other. He turned his head to smile at Joseph and was concerned to see that he seemed to have lapsed again into unconsciousness, his head lolling to one side.

The quivering cable had begun to lift the vehicle off the bank. The steel line was stretched as hard as a rod between the winch and the Land Rover and Shaun flinched as it made a sudden, jerky twitch. He wondered what would happen if it snapped. With anxious glances at Joseph, he continued plying the lever until his shoulders ached and the skin of his hands blistered.

Quite suddenly, it was over. The movement of the lever became rapidly easier as the weight on the end of the cable approached its point of balance. Old Laura teetered, tottered, then swayed over onto all four wheels with a rattle and a sigh. The two boys were too exhausted to cheer.

All Shaun wanted to do was to collapse in the soft sand and rest, but he was worried about Joseph and about the prospect of the old man's assailants returning.

Sam had gone over to where Joseph lay propped up against the bank and was fanning him with his hat. Shaun joined him and used more of the water, sponging Joseph's face and neck. Eventually he woke up again, but he seemed weaker than before and he was confused for a minute about where they were and what was happening.

Leaving Sam to care for Joseph, Shaun climbed into the driver's seat, found the ignition switch, took a deep breath and twisted it. Nothing. Not a whir, not a moan, not a grunt. He closed his eyes and breathed a little prayer before trying again. Not a sound. His shoulders sagged and he leaned his head wearily against the steering wheel. All right, he told himself, what would Dad do? Think first! No electricity to turn the starter motor. Battery. Maybe one of the leads came off in the crash.

Retrieving Joseph's tyre lever from the back, he began working to prise open the bonnet. It gave after a few good heaves and he climbed onto the roo-bar and looked into the engine bay. His heart sank. Both leads were firmly secured to the battery, but the battery itself was split from top to bottom on one side and all the fluid had drained out. It was totally useless. They were stranded.

Swallowing hard to control the lump of despair swelling in his throat, he walked slowly back to the others. He threw himself onto his back in the sand

and looked up through the leaves of the acacia tree. Why couldn't they just take off and fly away like the hawk he could see way up in the wide expanse of blue? Why couldn't it be that easy? Rolling over onto his side, he told Sam and Joseph about the battery.

'You boys get out of here.' Joseph was obviously in pain, but he tried to look cheerful. 'Get back to the motorbike and call the homestead on the radio. Your dad can come out in the truck and pick me up. Go on, I'll be OK.'

Shaun was not so sure. 'This valuable discovery of yours, is it at your camp?' Joseph nodded, face puckered with pain. 'Will those men find it?'

Joseph hesitated. 'They might,' he said, 'but I doubt if they will recognise it. It's not something they can just take away and sell.'

'Then we're not leaving you. If they don't find what they're looking for they might come back and try to make you tell them where it is. And if it turns out to be something they can't use, they might get angry and beat you up. Or worse. Dad knows we came to the gorge. When we don't get back he'll come looking for us.'

Joseph tried to argue with them, but he was too tired to put up a real fight. Shaun took up the tyre lever and sat down defiantly on the old man's right with the weapon clutched in his fist. Sam located the toolbox and, returning with an enormous spanner, deposited himself with equal determination on Joseph's left. There they sat for about five minutes until Sam began to chuckle.

'What's so funny?' growled Shaun, glaring across at him.

Sam's lips twisted in a wry smile. 'There are no bad guys on sheep stations,' he said.

14

Dead end

THE SUN CLIMBED HIGHER as the morning advanced.
The day was turning into a real scorcher and it soon
became apparent that the water they had brought
with them would not last long. Joseph always
travelled with a jerry can of water, but that was at
the camp. The canvas water bag attached to the
front of the Land Rover had suffered the same fate
as the tyre and the battery. They sat in silence, only
moving in order to stay in the shade as the sun
progressed across the steely oven of the sky. After
a while it seemed to Shaun that they had been sitting
there for ever and would be forevermore. Time
stood still.

Sam spoke, breaking the spell. 'If we had another
battery, could we start the engine?'

'Sure,' whispered Joseph weakly, 'but it would
have to be a car battery.' He chuckled painfully.

'Even if that battery was still in warranty, I can't imagine anyone coming out here to replace it.'

They were silent again for a long time, then Sam spoke again, tentatively. 'I saw something on TV once. A bloke was out in the desert and he got a car running with a torch battery.'

Shaun rolled his eyes. 'Don't be stupid! You can't run a car engine with a torch battery!'

'It's true,' protested Sam. 'It was one of those big square ones with two sort of spring things on top.'

Shaun started to argue, but Joseph cut across him excitedly. 'You know, you could be right! Those batteries are six volts. Just let me think. Yes, you wouldn't have enough current to operate the starter motor, but once the engine was turning over, six volts is probably enough to run the ignition. Sam, you're brilliant!'

The two boys nearly fell over each other in their eagerness to find the big red torch Joseph assured them was somewhere in the back of the vehicle. Eventually they tumbled back out through the tailgate waving their prize. There was a set of jumper leads in the toolbox and, following Joseph's instructions, they set about connecting one terminal of the battery to the Land Rover's high-tension coil and the other to a big bolt on the side of the motor. The battery itself they taped firmly in place with adhesive plaster from Joseph's first aid kit. They climbed out from under the bonnet and wiped their oily hands on their jeans. Shaun hoped it would work, but even if it didn't, at least it had kept them occupied for half an hour.

The next problem was to turn the engine over. As Joseph had pointed out, using the starter motor would have drained such a small battery in a matter of seconds. But, as he also pointed out, it was lucky the vehicle was a Land Rover: they came with a crank handle. Joseph was getting frustrated with just sitting and letting the boys do all the work. He tried to get up and hobble over to help them, but slumped to the ground again with a moan of agony. Shaun ran over to him and yelled at him, more in fear than anger, to stay put.

He examined the broken leg and was alarmed to see fresh, red blood showing through the old brown stains on the bandage. Not really knowing what else to do, he dived into the rucksack and brought out one of the shirts Sam had packed. Wrapping it around the bandaged wound, he tied it as tight as he could without hurting his old friend.

They found the crank handle clipped into position down beside the driver's seat. Inserting the end of it through the hole in the bumper and into its notch in the front of the engine, Shaun threw his weight against it. It would not budge. This was going to be harder than he had thought!

His father's voice echoed inside his head. Stop. Think. Of course! The car had been in gear when it crashed. He jumped into the cab and slipped the lever into neutral. He checked the ignition key. It was on. Back to the crank once more, this time with Sam helping. They had done it with the winch, so why not with the crank? Together they strained and it turned, a sudden jerk about halfway around, then seemed to stick again.

They heaved against it and it leapt another half-turn. This time the motor gasped and wheezed as though it was trying to fire. Again, and the old vehicle replied with a sputter and a cough. With what Shaun felt was his last shred of energy, they managed to wind the handle fully three revolutions without stopping. The engine shuddered and chugged, but kept on after the boys sank to the ground, exhausted. They shouted encouragement as old Laura fought for breath like an asthmatic pensioner. Gradually, she regained her composure and began to hum. It was a song sweeter than anything Shaun could remember.

After all they had accomplished, levering the mudguard away from the ruined tyre and changing the wheel seemed easy. Shaun had lost count of the times he had helped his father with that kind of thing. Joseph insisted on riding up front with the boys, even though he would not be able to drive and, with a little difficulty, they eventually had him seated.

While Shaun was making him as comfortable as he could, Sam wandered off. Shaun had to look for him and found him standing on the bank of the creek surveying the rugged ridges on either side of the valley.

He seemed not to hear when Shaun called him and, when Shaun climbed up beside him and touched him on the shoulder, he did not respond immediately but turned as though waking from sleep. Then he jumped lightly down into the creek bed and walked over to the Land Rover leaving Shaun to frown after him in perplexity.

Back in the driver's seat, Shaun hesitated with his hand on the gear lever. 'I reckon we should go north,' he said. 'The gorge crosses the boundary into Morton Vale. I've never been further than that, but I reckon there must be a way we can cut back through the hills to one of the homesteads, either Morton Vale or my place.'

Joseph opened his mouth, but it was Sam who spoke first. 'No. You can't get out that way. We've got to go back the other way, past the Turtleshell.'

'How would you know?' retorted Shaun. 'You've never been here before. Look, this is my land; I've lived here all my life. We'll go north.'

But Sam was insistent. 'You're wrong. If we go that way we'll be trapped. The hills close up over there somewhere like the bottom of a sack. That's where. . .' He hesitated.

'Where what? See, you don't know at all. I don't know why you're making all this up, but — '

'I'm not making it up!' Sam shouted and flung open the door to leap out, but Joseph gripped his arm and stopped him.

The prospector looked at Sam with a curious expression. 'How *did* you know that?' he asked.

'It's part of the Dreaming. My uncle told me about this place. At least I suppose it was the Turtleshell. There isn't another big rock like that around here, is there? One that looks like the top of a big man's bald head sticking up out of the ground?'

'No,' answered Joseph. 'This is the only one.' He turned to Shaun. 'He's quite right, you know. On the other side of the Morton Vale boundary the gorge curves around to the west, but the sides get closer together until they meet. There is a track through, but it hasn't been used for years.'

Shaun was getting impatient. 'There you are; there's a track. It's got to be worth a try. Better than meeting up with the blokes who shot at Joseph, anyway.' Sam didn't really like the decision, but he settled himself back in the seat and closed the door. Shaun had to stretch a bit to put the clutch to the floor and strain a bit to see properly out of the window. Essentially, though, it was not much different to driving the station ute and he had been doing that for several years now. In first gear, the old vehicle bumped along the dry watercourse to the crossing, then ground its way up the bank.

The track to the northern end of the gorge was rough and rutted, cut in places with steep-sided gullies. At times, Shaun ground the gears and spun the wheels as he negotiated the crossings, but his passengers were too preoccupied with their own problems to worry. Joseph's injured leg was obviously giving him pain with every bump and Sam was doing his best to keep the old man from bouncing around too much in the lurching cabin. Eventually, they came to the boundary of the property, marked by an old, sagging fence with barbed wire along the top. A rusted gate carried a faded and bullet-holed sign that proclaimed: *Moreton Vale — No Shooters!*

The gate had not been used for a long time and it took both the boys to drag it open wide enough to admit the Land Rover. Then they continued, the gorge curving gradually around to the left, the track getting harder to find amid bushes and floor-high, dry grass.

At one point, as they passed through a stand of mulga, they were confronted by a tree fallen across the track. It was too large to move by hand and Shaun feared that, if they tried to drag it out of the way with the vehicle, they might stall the engine and not be able to start it again, so he reversed back out of the trees and picked his way carefully through the scrub, skirting the thicket until he located the track again on the other side.

All the time, the high, rugged walls on their right and left came closer together. Eventually they rounded an outcrop and saw the end of the gorge. The ground rose in a series of small humps until it met the rock and it was between two of these humps that the track made its way upward. Water had been making its way downward by the same route for many years, it seemed, and the track resembled a pair of narrow, parallel creeks more than a road.

Shaun fought the steering wheel as Laura whined in low gear up to the granite wall and there he stopped. He looked at Joseph and Sam and knew from their faces that they agreed with him; there was no way even the most experienced driver could negotiate that path. It had been cut by a bulldozer into the seep side of a narrow gully. Once it must have been passable, but not any more. Parts of it had washed away and in other places rock slides had completely blocked it. Wearily, he put the Land Rover into reverse and backed slowly down to a place where he could turn around.

They held a council of war. Sam volunteered to climb through the pass and walk to Moreton Vale

Homestead, but Shaun and Joseph both knew it was too far. Joseph tried again to persuade the boys to drop him at the creek and go on foot to the motor-bike, but they both refused to leave him. Obviously they had no choice but to risk the run back to the exit at the southern end of the gorge. As they bumped back down towards the boundary fence, Shaun was silently thankful to Sam for not saying 'I told you so'.

Every minute they had wasted going north increased the chance that the men who had attacked Joseph might return to get him, but they had no alternative: they had to take the chance. When they reached the creek where Joseph had crashed and saw no sign of the gunmen or their car, Shaun dared to hope that they had left the gorge altogether.

15

Capture

ALTHOUGH IT WAS IN THE BOTTOM of the narrow valley, the Turtleshell emerged from the ground at a point that was higher than much of the surrounding land. The creek they had just left had to make a wide arc to get around the great dome and there was a good view up and down the valley from the place where the track passed close to the rock. They stopped there and the boys got out.

As he stared down the length of the gorge to the place where he knew they could cross the hills, Shaun wished they had thought to bring the binoculars down from the cave. They could see no telltale dust from the gunmen's car, so the only thing to do was to press on.

Walking back to the Land Rover, Shaun looked up at the sides of the Turtleshell, rising nearly vertically from the earth. He always felt a bit awestruck when he was this close to it. The material of which it was formed was different from the granite and quartz of the valley walls or the limestone that characterised the lower slopes and parts of the floor. It was smooth, almost glassy, and very hard. It was startlingly dark, not just a dark colour, but dark like the water at the bottom of a mine shaft: it seemed to swallow up the sunlight that fell on it. Nevertheless it always felt cool and, as he passed it, Shaun was tempted to put out his hand and touch it. Sam did so, and caressed the smooth surface almost reverently.

Slipping the Land Rover into gear, Shaun eased the vehicle over the crest, past the cool, dark flank of the Turtleshell and down the slope on the other side. He had begun to get the feel of old Laura now and, by the time the rock was a kilometre behind them, they were bowling along at quite a respectable rate. From time to time he glanced up to his left, trying to locate the cave. He knew pretty well where it was, but the sun was high and burning fiercely, throwing everything under the overhang into impenetrable shadow.

As they rounded a spur of the high rampart to their left, they could see where the track began to climb up to pass through a narrow opening between two high peaks. It was the way home and Shaun's heart began to race with anticipation. At the same time, however, Sam gripped his arm and pointed through the windscreen.

Off to the right from about the direction Joseph had described his camp to be, a pillar of dust rose into the air. It grew longer as the source of it moved across the valley towards the same pass. Shaun pressed harder on the accelerator pedal and the old vehicle protested loudly as it responded. If only they could make it to the pass before the ute, he was sure their high ground clearance and four-wheel-drive transmission would give them better speed across the rough terrain of the hills than the low-slung Ford.

The closer they got to their goal, the more apparent it became that the other vehicle would arrive first and cut them off. They bucked and bounced over the rutted track. Shaun was grimly conscious that the rough ride must be doing Joseph's broken leg no good, but he had no idea of the pain the old man was suffering until, glancing across, he saw him slumped ashen-faced against Sam. Sam, his arms wrapped tightly around Joseph to hold him up, shouted at Shaun to keep going. However, when finally the other vehicle reached the junction of the two tracks and turned towards them, Shaun slipped the gear lever into neutral and let the old Land Rover coast to a halt. They had lost the race. If the men started shooting at the vehicle to stop it again, he reasoned, this time someone might be killed.

Shaun was bitterly disappointed and too tired really to be afraid as the white Ford approached.

They had laboured long and hard, first to reach Joseph and then to rescue him, and they had nearly succeeded. He switched off the engine. The afternoon was wearing on and the sun struck hotly through Shaun's window.

Now that they were stationary, the heat in the small cab of the Land Rover was stifling and, as he waited for the gunmen to arrive, he leaned back in the seat and closed his eyes, hardly caring what they might do. When the ute did slide to a halt in front of them in a thick cloud of dust, he opened his eyes to watch the passenger leap out and swagger towards him, rifle hanging negligently from the crook of his arm.

What happened when the man reached the vehicle was actually quite funny. While he must have wondered at Joseph's ability to survive the crash, right the Land Rover all by himself and drive it to this spot, it obviously didn't occur to him that anything else could be the case. Perhaps the sun in his eyes and the dust of his own car's arrival prevented him from seeing clearly into the interior of the Land Rover.

Whatever he expected to see as he bent confidently to leer in the driver's window, it certainly was not a freckle-faced boy. His whiskered jaw dropped a few inches and Shaun could see his tongue sort of twitching as though it had lost its grip on whatever it was he was about to say. The triumphant gleam his eyes possessed when they appeared in the window faded to a puzzled haze and the creases above his dusty eyebrows deepened into furrows of amazement. Shaun smiled tiredly at him and bobbed his head politely. 'G'day!' he said.

For fully thirty seconds the man stared into the cab, trying to digest what he saw. Suddenly his mouth snapped shut and his head disappeared from the window like a goanna startled back into its burrow. He hurried over to the ute, looking back over his shoulder, and conferred hastily with his companion, waving his free hand and pointing at the Land Rover.

When next he approached, he seemed to have recovered his wits. He levelled the rifle at the boys and ordered them to get out. They obeyed. Joseph, close to collapse, they left propped up in the cabin. After peering suspiciously at the old prospector, their captor instructed them to move to the front of the vehicle. Only then did the second man climb from the Ford and stroll over to inspect them. He frowned and chewed on a match stick as he looked them up and down.

He was short and thick. A big floppy hat that had once been white shaded a pale face above a grubby tee-shirt and moleskin trousers that would never be white again. He looked for all the world like an overgrown toadstool.

'How the hell did you two get here?' he growled.

Shaun opened his mouth, but Sam was quicker. 'Shaun's dad brought us out here to camp for a few days,' he lied. 'He'll be picking us up the day after tomorrow.'

All the fear and anger Shaun had accumulated since they first saw the chase from the cave boiled over. 'You mongrel!' he shouted. 'We saw you shoot at him! You could have killed him! You were probably trying to, anyway!' Tears blinded him as he started forward in fury, oblivious to the ominous click of the rifle bolt. Sam grabbed him and spun him around, pushing him back against the Rover, shaking him until the pounding in his ears abated and he could think again.

'Shut up!' hissed his friend, urgency edging his voice. 'Right now they dunno what to do with us, but pull something like that again and they'll make up their mind quick smart!'

Toadstool stepped over and roughly dragged them apart. Grasping each one by a handful of hair, he propelled them to a spot some metres from the vehicles and told them to sit. Warning them not to move, he and his mate pulled Joseph from the Land Rover. He seemed to have lost consciousness again, and Shaun thought dully that it was probably a blessing: at least he couldn't feel anything. The men lowered Joseph none too gently into the back of the ute and Shaun started to his feet, but Sam put out his hand and prevented him. 'Not yet,' he said.

Next, Shaun and Sam were taken at gunpoint back to their vehicle and told to drive slowly along the track the Ford had arrived on until they reached Joseph's camp. They appeared to have no choice. Shaun explained about the battery and derived some satisfaction from watching the gunman labour over the crank handle. With the ute behind them, cutting off their escape, he turned the Land Rover off the main track and headed across into the shadow of the western wall of the gorge.

It was only a few minute's drive, but long enough for Sam to outline the plan he had been working on ever since they realised they had to turn south and risk capture. Whatever they did, he said, they must not let on that they had a motorbike and a radio a few kilometres away on the other side of the hills. Also, they had to stick to the story that they were due to be picked up in a couple of days. Saying Shaun's dad was picking them up would stop the men guessing about the bike and, if they thought they had a day or so to spare, they were less likely to do something desperate. Sam's reasoning sounded impressive and all Shaun could do was to hope he was right.

16

Escape

JOSEPH'S CAMPS WERE NEVER VERY NEAT, but this was a mess. Boxes and bags were scattered about indiscriminately, some broken open and their contents strewn over a wide area. A sack of flour had been cut open and emptied onto the ground. Packets of tea and sugar lay with broken surveying instruments and smashed bottles of chemicals among the rocks beside the track. There was only one oasis of order among the chaos: in a clear space under a large redgum stood three petrol cans and a card table.

The boys climbed down from the Land Rover as the ute drew up, and watched helplessly as Joseph's limp body was lifted from the back and carried over to the clearing. As the men laid him on the ground, Shaun bent anxiously over him, ignoring the gruff order to get away. The old man's breathing was shallow and irregular and the skin of his face looked thin and dry like old newspaper. There was a small spot of blood showing through the extra layer of cloth wrapped around the bandage on the injured leg.

Shaun stood up angrily. 'He needs a doctor! He'll die if you don't take him to a doctor. Don't you care?'

Toadstool grinned unkindly, revealing teeth as grubby as his moleskins. 'Don't you worry about him, sonny. Roly here'll fix him. Roly's good at fixing people, aren't you Roly?' There was no humour in Roly's answering laugh. He raised the rifle and shepherded the boys away from the clearing. Shaun flinched as Toadstool slapped Joseph several times on the cheek, but the old man did not respond.

Toadstool was unmistakably the leader of the pair. Approaching, he ordered Roly to make the old man comfortable in the shade and cool him down with some water from the ute. Then he turned and surveyed Shaun and Sam. Hooking his thumbs into the waistband of his trousers, he raised himself up and down several times on his toes while looking at them with squinted eyes and pursed lips. Finally he spoke.

'Look, you lads aren't a part of this. The old man has something we need and, soon as he comes round, we'll ask him where it is. Then Roly and me'll be off. Old man'll come with us, of course. Insurance, you might say. You have never seen us before and, if you know what's good for your friend, you'll have a lot of difficulty remembering what we look like.'

He caught Sam looking intently at the ute and chuckled. 'Don't worry about memorising numbers, matey. It's, ah, sort of borrowed.' He looked at the sky. 'Be getting dark before too long. Make yourselves useful. Light a fire and fix us something to eat.'

Sam scouted around and salvaged tins of spaghetti, baked beans and vegetables from the litter of the camp while Shaun cleared a space and piled dry leaves and sticks inside a circle of stones. His father had always been adamant about observing the fire-ban season, but Shaun reasoned that if he could create some smoke, Dad would head for it if he came looking for the boys. If they could keep it burning into the night, that would be an effective beacon too, clearly visible from the pass. The task of collecting fuel and constructing the fire, getting it going and heating up the food occupied the two for a while, helping to keep their minds off the danger they were in.

By the time the group had eaten in tense silence, the sun had set, plunging the bottom of the gorge into deep shadow. Only the peaks of the eastern rim were visible, glowing red-hot like the jagged edge of oxy-cut metal. Roly tossed blankets to the boys and

asked if they wanted a bedtime story, laughing harsh-
ly at their glares.

Shaun hoped that he was too busy thinking up
nasty comments to worry that they spread their
blankets further from the fire than he would expect
on a night that promised to be chilly. He hoped also
that neither of the men would notice how close he
settled down to a long, boy-sized pile of firewood he
had collected earlier in the evening, or think it strange
that he should jam his hat onto his head as he
wrapped himself in the blanket.

Half an hour passed, during which Shaun's hip
and shoulder became progressively more uncomfort-
able. The ground was hard and covered with small
stones. He moved his head slightly to look at Sam.
He saw only the gleam of his teeth in the firelight as
his friend grinned encouragement and the glint of his
eyes as he winked across the metre of ground that
separated them. Time crawled by and eventually
their two captors settled for the night, Roly wriggling
into a bulky sleeping bag, Toadstool throwing a log
onto the fire and seating himself on an upturned crate
with the rifle resting across his knees.

Shaun's anger rose in his throat as he saw that they
simply left Joseph lying unconscious where they had
placed him, near the fire but uncovered under the
clear sky. Everything in him wanted to go over and
attend to the old man, but he forced himself to close

his eyes and blot out the sight, concentrating on what he was about to do. Without medical help, he was certain Joseph would die and Sam's plan seemed the only way to get it.

Shaun's body ached unbearably and he counted silently to five thousand as the stars crept imperceptibly across the sky. He could see the Southern Cross through the branches of the redgum and, further to the right, Canopus shining brilliantly against the silver dusting of the Milky Way. Eventually he turned to Sam again and mouthed, 'Now?', but Sam shook his head slowly and looked meaningfully across the fire at Toadstool. Sure enough, their guard stood up a few minutes later and stretched, then wandered over to where they lay.

The two closed their eyes and lay still as he approached and Shaun could feel him standing over them, staring down at them for a long minute before walking a few yards into the scrub to relieve himself. The sound of it made Shaun aware of just how full his own bladder was, but he held his breath and waited: to get up now would just mean prolonging the time they needed to convince Toadstool they were properly asleep.

The man finally settled himself back on the box, after stoking up the fire, and Shaun was momentarily startled to feel Sam's touch on his shoulder. Sam had silently wriggled close enough to be heard as he breathed, 'Now. He's just checked us and, with the fire so high, he can't see us easily from the other side.' Shaun hesitated, unwilling to commit himself to the dangerous course of action he was about to take, and Sam touched him again. 'I'll go if you like. I won't stand out so much in the dark.' He flashed another of his now-frequent grins. 'I am black, you know.'

Shaun nearly laughed out loud. He grinned back and shook his head. They had discussed this point in the Land Rover on the way to the camp: despite his uncle's stories, Sam would have difficulty finding his way to the place they had left the bike and, even if he found it, he didn't know how to use the radio. Also, if nobody was listening at the other end, he would have to ride the bike back to the house to raise the alarm. It had to be Shaun.

Slowly, soundlessly, Shaun eased the blanket off his body, folding it back over the mound of firewood behind him. The operation took forever and all the time his aching muscles screamed out for him to get up and stretch. Next, he took his hat off and, turning slowly towards the firewood, laid it against the end of the mound. It didn't look much like a sleeping boy from this close, he decided, but hopefully from the other side of the fire the view was less clear.

Rolling onto his belly, he inched himself forward, using his elbows and knees, towards the deeper shadows of the bushes further from the firelight. As he passed Sam, his friend reached out and gripped his wrist. The dark eyes as he looked into them held a concern that was mirrored in the strong grasp and the whispered message: 'Good luck!'

Progress was slow and painful, with scratches and bruises accumulating on his hands, knees and elbows, not to mention the discomfort of the sand that found its way into his shirt and grass seeds that lodged themselves in his trousers and socks. Once he nearly screamed aloud as a many-legged something landed in his hair and crawled down his neck onto his back. He lay still for minutes, sweating, controlling the urge to leap up and brush it off, but he felt nothing more and convinced himself that it had gone.

Crawling forward again, he considered that really he had the easiest job: at least he was moving, and away from the danger at that. Sam had to endure hours of waiting, pretending to be asleep, wondering what would happen if the men discovered the deception.

Eventually, a few hundred metres from the camp, he intercepted the track that ran towards the pass out of the gorge. Raising himself on his knees, he peered back over the level of the scrub and decided it was safe to stand upright. It was heavenly to stretch and ease his muscles (and his bladder) and his spirits rose as he jogged down the track towards the far side of the gorge. Alternately jogging and walking, he found he could make surprisingly good time and he reached the intersection of the two tracks where they had been captured just as the moon rose, large and yellow, over the rugged rock wall ahead of him.

The track began to climb and Shaun began to realise just how dreadfully tired he was. He had been going since sunrise, first climbing across that ghastly cliff face, riding the rockslide down the crevice and hiking across the gorge to Joseph's crashed vehicle, then having to right and start the Land Rover and drive it to the camp. Now he had crawled and walked and jogged some five kilometres back across the gorge to begin the climb up to the pass. In all that time, although he had eaten and drunk, it was not really enough to make up for the heat of the day and the strain of fear and worry he had endured.

He found as he plodded upward towards the vee of the pass etched against the starry sky that his legs became heavier and required more effort to move with each step. Finally he only progressed by counting aloud and willing one foot after another to place itself forward and take his weight.

Every time he was tempted to sink down in despair and abandon himself to tears, he pictured Joseph lying under the stars with his face pale and creased, and he found strength from somewhere to press on. As he neared the top, he found to his surprise that he had been humming a tune under his breath and marching in time to it. Recognising it as a song he had learnt at Sunday school, he matched the tune with words: 'Faith is like a muscle, use it and it will grow. . .' He certainly needed muscles now, with Sam and Joseph depending on him, perhaps for their lives. 'When a mountain comes up, face it square and strong. . .'[1] One foot in front of the other, on he went, and the song seemed to help.

Suddenly he was at the top. The panorama of bluebush plains shone silver in the moonlight, broken in patches by dark clumps of mulga. It all looked clean and fresh, and somehow thrilling, magical; familiar yet strangely different as though he were seeing it for the first time, or through new eyes. The clear, star-dusted sky sucked heat from him and he shivered violently, as much from exhaustion as from cold. He stomped his feet a few times, slapped his arms around his body to warm himself, and began a shambling trot down the far side of the pass.

The final stage of his journey, as the track led him diagonally across the face of the hill, took place in a sort of dreamlike exhilaration. He could hardly feel the jarring of his feet on the ground, although the sound of it filled his head. His breath burned in his chest, whether from heat or cold he could not tell, and for some reason tears streamed down his cheeks, obscuring his vision so that it seemed to make no difference whether his eyes were open or shut. When they were shut, although he knew dimly that he was likely to trip on the uneven track or run off it into the scrub, he felt almost as though he were flying. When his eyes were open, the moonlight above and the bluebush spread below merged into a single, incredibly beautiful silver haze that filled his vision as the pounding of his feet filled his ears.

How Shaun knew to stop at the tree where they had left the motorbike, he never worked out. He only knew that he opened his eyes to find he had finished running and was standing by the machine holding on to the handlebar. He had no idea how long he had been there, although his even breathing and quiet heartbeat suggested it had been some minutes. It took him a moment more to remember why he was here, and what he should do next. When the memory came and with it jumbled visions of shooting, a crash, a blood-soaked bandage and two men at a wrecked camp, his stomach churned until he was almost sick. He clutched the bike weakly until the spell passed, then began picking at the straps securing the sacking-wrapped radio to the handlebars.

Fumbling, almost dropping the radio, he extended the aerial and turned the switch. He depressed the talk button and called, and was almost overwhelmed with relief when his father's voice, edged with worry, answered immediately. He tried to relate what had happened, but the words came out all confused. Finding a moment when Shaun released the button, Dad told him to explain exactly where he was and to stay there. The firm, calm voice restored some order to Shaun's whirling thoughts and he was able to reply coherently. He was also thinking clearly enough now to recognise through the static of his father's transmission the characteristic sound of a radio operating from a moving vehicle: Dad must have been already on his way to the gorge when Shaun called.

His task over, the last of Shaun's energy drained away and he slid down to the ground, huddled against the back wheel of the bike, head bent, arms wrapped tightly around his knees, shivering uncontrollably. He didn't notice the headlights or the anxious calling as his father drew up beside him. The first thing he knew was strong arms lifting him into the truck and his mother's voice coaxing him to drink from the steaming cup she held to his lips.

17

The treasure

SHAUN OPENED HIS EYES. The room was warm and bright with the sunlight that streamed through the window to his left. Outside he could see part of the pepper tree and inside his eye followed the wall around, noting the familiar posters, bookshelves, models. A gentle touch on his hair made him turn his head to find his mother smiling down at him.

'Welcome back to the land of the living,' she said.

Shaun frowned, trying to remember. 'Sam?'

'Sound asleep in the guest room.'

Memory crystallised with a jolt and he tried to sit up. 'Joseph?'

His mother gently pressed his head back onto the pillow. 'He's safe. He's in hospital, but the doctor says he'll recover. You're heroes, you know. He wouldn't have lasted another day out there.'

Shaun was still confused. 'Where's Dad? What

happened to those two men? How did Sam and Joseph get away?'

'Hold your horses, Shaun. Dad's out at the gorge with the police. As for the rest of the story, what say we wake Sam and have some breakfast first. Even if it is past lunchtime!' She stepped out into the passage, but a moment later her face appeared around the doorpost. 'By the way, happy birthday!'

As Mum was waking Sam, Shaun heard engines in the distance. He slid out of bed and padded to the back door in pyjamas and bare feet. A convoy of three police vehicles, led by the station truck, hove into view and turned into the yard amid clouds of dust, welcomed exuberantly by Gyp. The occupants all climbed out and walked to the house, wiping foreheads on sleeves and slapping dust off uniforms. They assembled on the verandah and Dad, seeing Shaun, and Sam who had joined him at the door, called them out into the midst of an admiring crowd where hair was ruffled, backs slapped and hands shaken.

'Got 'em, thanks to you blokes,' said a sergeant.

'Where are they?' asked Sam.

'In the paddy wagon,' replied the sergeant, indicating over his shoulder with his thumb.

Mum had appeared at the door. 'Bit warm in there on a day like this, isn't it?'

The police sergeant laughed. 'Let 'em sweat.

That's what they'll be doing in court.'

After arranging for the boys to make statements in town later in the day, the police contingent strolled back to their vehicles and departed, revving and roaring into the distance. Sam, Shaun and his parents went back into the kitchen where the boys attacked a mound of toasted cheese and ham sandwiches. At last, the four sat around the table and swapped stories. It was then that Shaun learned what had happened after his trek across the gorge and through the pass.

Dad had left him in Mum's care with a pile of blankets and a thermos flask of hot soup while he took the truck into the gorge to find Sam and Joseph. As he neared the camp, he had seen the ute's head-lights come on, the vehicle moving off to the south in a great hurry.

He had debated whether to chase it, not knowing whether they had taken anyone with them, but had next seen Sam running towards him down the track, waving his arms. Sam led him to where Joseph lay and they had lifted the old prospector into the truck and brought him back to the homestead, picking up Shaun and his mother on the way. From there, after phoning ahead, Dad had taken Joseph in to the hospital and returned with the police who had as-sembled in the meantime. They had arrived at Turtleshell homestead at dawn and headed out to the gorge where apparently they had no difficulty in picking up Toadstool and Roly.

'What I can't understand,' said Shaun when the story was finished, 'is why they were still there. I mean, that track turns west once it leaves the gorge and ends up meeting the Barrier Highway, doesn't it? They could have been in Broken Hill by the time the police got here.'

Dad let Sam answer. 'Remember those three petrol cans? Well, the men jumped up and ran to the ute as soon as they saw your dad's headlights coming. They almost took off without the cans, but Roly shouted that the tank was nearly empty and ran back to get them.'

'So?' asked Shaun. 'That would have been enough to get them anywhere they wanted to go.'

Sam was enjoying himself. 'Well, you remember all the packets of food and stuff lying around? While you were busy building the fire and the men were trying to wake up Joseph, I emptied a packet of sugar into the petrol tins. I saw that. . .'

'I know,' interrupted Shaun, laughing. 'You saw that once on TV.'

*   *   *

Shaun blinked as they stepped out of the police station into the glare of the late afternoon sun. It had been a strangely tiring experience describing their adventure in minute detail for the benefit of a grey typewriter. Looking across at Sam while they walked down the verandahed footpath towards the hospital, Shaun saw signs of strain on his face, too.

However, the thought that occupied his mind as he walked beside his parents was about the names. The police sergeant had shown them the charge sheets prepared for Toadstool and Roly. Shaun couldn't get over the fact that such poisonous characters could have harmless names like Adam Lloyd Johnson and Roland John McEwen. He shook his head in wonderment as they turned in at the hospital entrance.

Both boys were shocked by the sight of Joseph. He was washed, combed and shaven, but his face was nearly as pale as the pillowslip against which it rested. He was asleep, but his eyelids twitched as though he were having a bad dream. A plastic bag on a tall stand by the bedside dripped clear fluid through a tube into his arm. Shaun could only bear to watch for a minute before turning away. Then they headed down the hall to an office where a doctor examined the boys, peering into their eyes and ears, listening to their chests and finally pronouncing them fit and well despite their ordeal.

The doctor said that Joseph should be well enough to sit up and have visitors the next day. The evening was warm so they ate fish and chips on the grass by the rotunda in the centre of the town before driving to a motel for the night. Shaun was asleep almost as soon as his head hit the pillow, but not before he heard Dad telling someone who knocked at the door to try the police station and see how they felt about talking to newspaper bloodhounds in the middle of the night.

Next morning, Shaun and Sam ate breakfast in bed, served by an admiring manageress who had apparently heard something of their story. They felt much brighter as they dressed and went out to visit Joseph. They approached the hospital room with some trepidation, but were delighted and relieved to find Joseph awake, propped up on pillows, smiling at them with something of his old humour. He could remember little of the events following his rescue from the creek bed, so the story was recounted again, this time with a growing audience of patients and hospital staff.

When Shaun reached the part where he made it to the bike and radioed for help, bated breath was exhaled noisily and someone clapped. As Sam glee-fully told of spiking the petrol with sugar, the room erupted into gales of laughter. Finally, amid whispered warnings of 'Matron!' and 'Look out, here she comes!', the crowd dispersed and the five of them were left alone.

Dad laid his hand gently on Joseph's shoulder and said, 'Well, you old Sundowner, I hope it was worth all the trouble. What was it you found out there that was so damn valuable, anyway?'

'Give me my pants and I'll show you,' grinned the prospector. They located the dusty, worn trousers and Joseph fished in one of the pockets, his hand emerging closed around something, and gestured for Sam to wheel the overbed table up where he could reach it. He placed whatever it was on the white laminex top and kept it covered for a moment while his eyes sparkled to see the suspense he was creating.

He lifted his hand to reveal three small rocks, all different. One looked like a piece of the quartz that was common throughout the gorge, with a lavender-coloured, pencil-shaped crystal embedded in it. Another was a smooth, lumpy pebble, dark red-brown like a piece of kidney. The third was an almost perfect cube of translucent crystal, shaded a delicate rosy pink.

'Very pretty,' said Mum, 'but what are they?'

Joseph lined them up and pointed to them each in turn: 'Tourmaline, haematite, flourite,' he announced gravely, as though making a highly significant statement. Amused by their bewildered silence, he continued as though lecturing his students. 'The Turtleshell is a volcanic intrusion, where molten lava forced its way up through weaknesses in the overlying strata millions of years ago. The rock all around got pretty darned hot while all that was going on, although the further it was from the lava, the cooler it was. Without going into the process in detail, different ores were formed at different temperatures depending on their distance from the source of the heat. The sequence of minerals like these that I found along the western wall of the gorge seems to indicate that there could be sizable deposits of copper, lead, zinc and iron not too far down all along the gorge. With any luck there might be silver, too.'

'Is that what those men were after?' Shaun asked.

'Well, I don't know what they thought I had found, but it would take a few million dollars to set up a mining operation, always assuming that the deposits were proven.' Joseph chuckled. 'I doubt whether they had that sort of money in their pockets.'

All through the conversation, Sam was uncharacteristically quiet. Now he spoke. 'If a big company did mine that stuff, how would they do it?' Some quality of his voice caused Joseph to look at him pensively before answering.

'If the deposits were reasonably close to the surface, as I suspect they are, it would be open-cut. That means they would use big machines to dig away all the earth that presently forms the floor of the gorge until they reached the ore body, then they'd blast it out with explosives.' He studied Sam's dark eyes thoughtfully for a moment, then said to the others, 'I wonder if you people could leave us for a while. I think there's something Sam would like to discuss with me.'

*   *   *

The lizard lay immobile. It could have been an outcrop from the native limestone, or a piece of dead wood fallen from the tree that shaded it. Only its leathery flanks moved rhythmically as it breathed, and its dark tongue flicked intermittently between tiny, armour-plated lips. From beneath ancient brows, its bright eyes considered the two boys. One was sandy-haired and freckled, the other dark-skinned, with unruly black curls. They sat side by side on the stony hilltop looking out over timeless plains toward ragged peaks on the southern horizon. The lizard drew delicate, transparent membranes across the shiny black jewels that were its eyes and dozed.

Shaun's birthday had been and gone. He did feel different, but not because of one day. It wasn't just the adventure in the gorge that had changed him, either: it had begun before that. He had grown a year older that day at the dump when he had decided to act like a friend to Sam whether he felt it or not. His instinct was right — the feelings had followed. He was glad his prayer to be rid of Sam hadn't been answered. What had Mum said? Thank God for the times he gives you what you need instead of what you ask for. And make the rest up as you go along. Somehow, now, school in Adelaide didn't seem so daunting.

Sam spoke. 'I'm going to miss all this.'

'There's plenty of land at Leigh Creek.'

'It's not the same. This is my land.'

'You can visit me.'

'You'll be at school most of the time.'

'So will you. Come in the holidays.'

Sam looked across at Shaun and smiled. 'I'd like that.'

Shaun sat silently for a time. He wasn't sure whether to voice the question that was on his mind. 'Why are you and your mum going back to him if he beats you up all the time?'

'He says he's going to stop. He says he's not drinking any more.'

'Do you believe him?'

Sam looked away to the horizon. 'He's my dad,' he said.

There was one solitary cloud, very white and unbelievably solid-looking, almost directly overhead. It cast a distinct shadow on the ground not far from the hill they shared. Shaun watched it move slowly eastward until it was lost from sight behind them.

'You never told me what you said to Joseph the other day at the hospital.'

Sam hesitated. 'Dreaming stuff. I told him the story my uncle told me about the gorge and the

Turtleshell. That's not its real name, you know. I don't know if I should have told him, but I did.'

'Will you tell me the story?'

Sam picked up a small rock and turned it over in his fingers, examining it. 'Dunno. One day, maybe.'

'So what did Joseph say?'

'He said he would talk to my mother when she gets here tomorrow. When he's a bit better, he'll go down to Adelaide and talk to my uncle. He said it might be possible to stop the mining company from digging up the gorge. I hope so.'

'So do I,' agreed Shaun.

Shaun closed his eyes and listened to the symphony of wind and grass, soaking up the warmth of the sun and the smell of the dust. He felt as though nothing could disturb the perfection of their hilltop. Sam had managed to touch some source of strength and peace through their adventure in the gorge. A new person was emerging from the hard shell of the boy Shaun had met only weeks earlier. Shaun himself had grown a year older and found a friend.

He smiled to himself. Not a bad birthday present really, when he came to think about it.

Endnote:

1. Copyright 1985, Mandy Dyson, 'Faith is like a muscle'